His Eyes Roamed Over Her in Bold Possessiveness . . .

He stroked her cheek, let his hand rest a moment on the pulse of her throat. Then he brought her into his arms, framing her face with long, surprisingly strong fingers as he bent to kiss her. The kiss began light, gay, and then changed, his lips moving on hers, lingering, hungry, insistent, making her blood race and giving her a light-headed feeling that left her with no strength. It was then that she knew nothing else mattered, nothing else was as important as remaining in the warm, loving shelter of his arms. . . .

More Romance from SIGNET

Enchanted Journey

By

Kristin Michaels

A SIGNET BOOK

NEW AMERICAN LIBRARY

TIMES MIRROR

NAL BOOKS ARE ALSO AVAILABLE AT DISCOUNTS IN BULK
QUANTITY FOR INDUSTRIAL OR SALES-PROMOTIONAL USE.
FOR DETAILS, WRITE TO PREMIUM MARKETING DIVISION,
NEW AMERICAN LIBRARY, INC., 1301 AVENUE OF THE
AMERICAS, NEW YORK, NEW YORK 10019.

 SIGNET TRADEMARK REG. U.S. PAT. OFF. AND FOREIGN COUNTRIES
REGISTERED TRADEMARK—MARCA REGISTRADA
HECHO EN CHICAGO, U.S.A.

SIGNET, SIGNET CLASSICS, MENTOR, PLUME AND MERIDIAN BOOKS
are published by The New American Library, Inc.,
1301 Avenue of the Americas, New York, New York 10019

FIRST SIGNET PRINTING, AUGUST, 1977

1 2 3 4 5 6 7 8 9

PRINTED IN THE UNITED STATES OF AMERICA

*To my good companions
of the Yucatán trip
and especially my roommate and leader,
Barbara de Montes*

I

The silent underground air of the caverns was humid, so heavy that it seemed to press clammily against Tory Stephens, but she still felt a strange chill at the way Brandy gazed at the enthroned jaguar, the carved heads, and the small figures centered around the massive pinnacle jutting up from a higher mound of the cave floor.

This was the holy of holies, the hidden secret of the narrow caverns, vaulted chambers, and broad passages that they and the rest of the Wings tour had followed. Everyone, understandably, was eager to see the Cave of Balankanche, sealed a thousand years before by priests. But the rest of the group had gone on, long ago, it seemed to Tory. And Brandy still lingered, so absorbed in the sanctuary that she was afraid to hurry him, even though he was the man she was to marry before the end of the year.

"At Christmastime," he'd decreed, laughing as he swept her into his embrace once she'd given the answer he'd been justifiably sure of. Who wouldn't be captured by Brandon Sherrod if he set his

1

agile mind and almost frightening will on it? "You'll be the rarest present I could ever have."

Tilting her face up, he'd stroked her hair back and murmured, with a look in his eyes that made her feel as if she were melting in wild sweetness, "I've known many women, Victoria. Too many, I was beginning to think, to settle for any one. But you're unique, from that silky cloud of black hair to those slanting changeable green eyes that can't keep me from looking at your delicious mouth."

Nice to hear him say it, but she knew she was nothing special. There were thousands of prettier girls, more intelligent ones, and she had no unusual talents, but from the day Brandy had walked into her aunt's rare-book shop, where she'd worked part-time during high school and college and full-time since, he'd seemed to find her worth his attention.

How old was he? Tory wondered, watching his proud, rather craggy profile in the soft luminosity of the small light bulbs. It was typical of Brandy that he'd never told her, and she hadn't felt comfortable about asking. From different things he'd said she knew he was at least in his mid-thirties.

"Isn't he a little old for you?" Elspeth, her aunt, had worried when Tory began seeing Brandy three or four times a week. When Tory looked surprised and indignant, Elspeth patted her hand. "Never mind, honey. Reckon I just hate to lose the best help I've ever had."

This trip was a thank-you to Aunt Elspeth,

though there was no way to thank her for loving and taking in her dead sister's daughter ten years ago, when Tory was eleven. Both her parents had died instantly in a car wreck. Elspeth had come to Washington for the funeral and then taken a dazed, grief-stricken child home with her to Dallas. Though Tory's father, a well-known lawyer, had left a comfortable estate and Elspeth did well to make expenses from the shop she loved, Tory's aunt had refused to draw from the money except for Tory's college education.

When Tory turned twenty-one that spring and assumed control of the estate, the first thing she'd done was make reservations for this birding tour to Yucatán. It was the kind of small luxury her aunt had forgone to rear her, and Tory wanted mightily to give Elspeth the kind of trip she'd wistfully dreamed of. She belonged to about every nature and conservationist group known to man, many of which sponsored tours all over the world. After artfully testing her aunt's reactions to an African journey, or Alaska and the Pribilofs, or the Andes, or the British Isles, Tory found it was the prospect of sighting birds among Mayan ruins and rain forests that most excited her aunt. So, a month ago, she'd bestowed the itinerary and confirmed reservations on her aunt along with a book on Mexican birds, a Spanish phrase book, and a paperback edition of John Stephen's 1843 classic, *Incidents of Travel in Yucatán.*

At first Aunt Elspeth declared it was too expensive, Tory mustn't squander her inheritance that way, and besides, who'd mind the shop? Tory produced the answer to that, Helen Marcus, a library-sciences major who had helped occasionally in the shop, browsed a lot, and knew the stock as well as being thoroughly trustworthy.

Aunt Elspeth wavered, plainly torn between the delights of the trip and responsibility to prevent Tory's wild spending. Then with a look of mingled tragedy and triumph, she exclaimed, "Brandon won't like it! He'll never let you out of his sight for three weeks!"

"Fudge!" said Tory. "He doesn't own me."

"Have you told him about this—this plot?"

"No, but—"

Elspeth gave a nod of gloomy satisfaction. "You know he won't approve. In your bones, you know it."

"Double fudge," said Tory, but she'd been apprehensive when she told him and greatly surprised when, after a silence, he inclined his silvery-gold head in approval.

"An excellent idea, Victoria. That part of Mexico fascinates me. I've been there often, you know, buying for my clients. Tours aren't my thing, but I rather think I'll sign on for this one and combine business with pleasure." At her amazed look, he laughed. "Don't worry, love. When I undertake to be part of a group, I manage very well."

And he had, charming the ladies and appearing to know something about the business each man was in or had retired from. He was the only person with a private room, but since he was also the only unmarried man besides Theron Powers, the guide, that privacy was not held against him.

Tory roomed with Elspeth, of course, but usually sat with Brandy on the chartered bus that had met them at Mérida airport. Elspeth was having a great time moving around and chatting with other people, comparing life lists and establishing affinities. Though a few couples like the Bowdries and Cunninghams made it politely clear that they were *together* and preferred to be alone as much as a tour permitted, most of the others fell into the friendly camaraderie of people sharing bird-walks at six and ten in the morning and late in the afternoon, interspersed with drives to the next site on a pink, purple, and gold bus named Dina that had frequent troubles with both air-conditioning and rest room. As sunburn, insect bites, swollen feet, and Montezuma's revenge took their toll, mutual advice and sharing of medicaments forged deeper bonds so that there was collective worry over whether plump Mildred Halliday could make it over certain trails; whether Gaye Burns, an amateur botanist, had seen a particularly lovely flower; or what Etheridge Martin, an ascetic Boston vegetarian, could find to eat at an all-seafood place.

Theron, a lean weathered man with dancing blue eyes and a sprinkling of white in black hair, was a freshly retired biology professor with an easy way of keeping his group together without making anyone feel either pushed or delayed. There were six older single women on the trip besides Elspeth, all of them widows, and they seemed to have an unusual number of questions for Theron, who gave detailed thoughtful answers when he knew and admitted when he didn't.

"Isn't he nice?" Tory impulsively asked her aunt one day when Theron had spent twenty minutes convincing an almost hysterical Anne Myers that a bump on her arm wasn't a fatal spider bite.

Elspeth had snorted, a strange sound from such a petite delicate woman who had scarcely a wrinkle for all her fifty-odd years. "Something has to be wrong with a man as attractive as that who's never married."

Tory gasped. It wasn't like her usually amiable kinswoman to prejudge someone, but Tory decided against inquiring if Elspeth cared to be appraised by the same rule since she, too, was attractive and had never married.

"Well," said Tory peaceably, "we'll probably learn all of each other's deep secrets during this tour such as why the Bowdries are so standoffish." But she wondered why her aunt was so hostile to the amiable tour leader and had become predictably sure to contradict his tentative identifications of poorly seen birds.

"I think that's a turquoise-browed motmot," he'd decided that morning after watching a bird perversely flirting at them from behind heavy leaf cover.

"I think it's an immature male blue-crown," Elspeth claimed.

Theron shrugged and grinned. "Would you

believe an irridescent curve-billed whatnot in juvenile plumage?"

The rest of the group tittered, but Elspeth gave him an outraged glare and fell back to the end of the file of birders.

"He's an arrogant condescending creature and I hope he breaks his binoculars!" she hissed in Tory's ear.

Tory gave her aunt a stare of bewilderment but didn't argue. Why had Elspeth taken this inexplicable aversion to the poor man, he had plenty of friendly attention.

And now he must be wondering where two missing members of his party were. It must have been at least fifteen minutes, though it seemed longer, since the group had left the sanctuary. By now they should be back in the sweet fresh moving air and sunlight.

Tory cleared her throat. "Brandy," she ventured.

He turned, his face changing as if emerging from a trance. "Bless you, darling! I just saw all these marvelous things and floated off. Come, let's catch up with the others before Theron has a search on."

He slipped his hand under her arm, but took a long last look back at the ancient images, the magnificent jaguar. "What a waste," he muttered as they reached a place where they had to go one by one. "Priceless treasures just sitting there."

"People get to see them," Tory protested. "And the Mayans must be proud to have the shrine the way it was before the Spaniards came."

Brandy's tone was dry. "Treasures belong to those who'll savor and guard them, keep them safe from careless handling and gawping by—"

He hesitated and Tory filled in. "The common herd? Good heavens, Brandy, that's a medieval way to think."

"Perhaps I am medieval," he said grimly. "At any rate, as you know, only my closest friends can view my private collection. I don't want what I treasure to be seen and touched by the public, and even if you think it quaint, my dear, you'd better accept that about me."

Something in his tone made her glance around, meet silvery eyes that roamed over her in bold possessiveness. He brought her into his arms, framed her face with long surprisingly strong fingers, and kissed her slowly till she felt weak, unable to stand without his support.

It was always this way with Brandy: his appeal was devastating, causing much different sensations than those evoked by any young man she'd ever known. Sometimes she felt possessed, as if a Merlin-like enchanter had walked into her life and taken it over. Brandy, with his fit, tanned body, lean face, and startling eyes and hair would stand out anywhere. Added to his appearance was casual elegance, a sophistication that approached world-weariness. Any woman would be flattered to attract him.

But do I really know him? Tory wondered after he'd released her and they moved again through the cavern. Is he kind? Will he want children? How will he act when I make mistakes?

It was one thing to be courted by such a man, another to contemplate living with him day after day. He was a perfectionist and Tory knew all too well that she was what her aunt called the three I's: impulsive, impractical, and idealistic. She hoped Brandy's expectations would help her amend the first two faults, but she really never wanted to be what most people called realistic.

Sliding down rough stone steps through a narrow passage, Tory had to concentrate on footing and not bumping her head till they emerged into the broad chamber that led through increasingly better air and light up to the entrance overhung with vines.

"Here you are," said Theron, rising from the circle of limestone that surrounded the cave's mouth. He looked harassed, and sure enough, Elspeth was perched near him, bird book in hand and truculent gleam in her hazel eyes. "Anyone want a bottled drink before we go? We'll lunch at Cancún, but that's quite a distance."

Brandy offered Tory a drink from his silver hip flask, but she didn't care for the taste of a Bloody Mary that early in the day and followed the group to the thatched caretaker's cottage.

Most of the bottled drinks were poisonous shades of green, orange, and cerise. Tory selected one of milder hue and found it pleasantly apple-flavored though oversweet. She was admiring the way palm fronds had been fitted securely on the peeled boughs of the room without the use of cords or any fastenings when Theron asked them to finish quickly and board Dina.

Narciso, the driver, a handsome young Mayan with broad cheekbones and black hair and eyes, always helped the women into the bus. It seemed to Tory that he held her arm a bit longer and more caressingly than was necessary, but his eyes were so merry and his *"¿Cómo está usted?"* so softly musical that she always smiled back and said, *"Bueno, gracias. ¿Y usted?"*

As always, this reply seemed to send him into a fit of laughter, though he composed himself and decorously replied, *"Muy bien, gracias,"* before he lent his hand and smile to hefty Mildred Halliday. Brandy was behind her, and Tory caught a glimpse of his frown, went back to her seat with an apprehensive feeling.

~ II ~

This was justified for, as soon as Brandy settled in the aisle seat beside her, he studied her for a few interminable seconds and then sighed. "Tory, love, I don't know how to say this. Your genuine friendliness and simplicity are part of your charm. But you shouldn't encourage bus drivers to languish over your hand."

"Languish?" Tory sparked at the word. "Narciso helps all the women. I certainly hope you're not a snob, Brandy. I could never stand it."

Lifting his silvery eyebrows, Brandy caught her hands, which she had unconsciously made into fists, gripped them, and smiled, shaking his shining head. "Forgive me, sweet. I shouldn't have taken that tone. But I have to make you understand. Do you remember Browning's 'My Last Duchess'?"

"Of course, but—"

" 'She had a heart too easily made glad,' " Brandy quoted. " 'Too easily impressed. . . . She loved whate'er she looked on and her looks went everywhere.' "

Remembering the arrogant, possessive noble's

confession—or boast, which was it?—Tory continued involuntarily, " 'Then all smiles ceased together.' Oh, Brandy, that's just overheated poet's imagining! How could any man kill a woman he loved because she was kind and happy and liked people?"

He regarded her somberly. The strange usually mirrorlike color of his eyes now seemed like shadow on snow. "There are men who can't share the woman they love." His hand closed over hers, slipped up her wrist, sending waves of tingling awareness through her . . . and a kind of warning. "I'm one of them, Victoria."

"You can't own people anymore." Joking to soften her words, she tried to elude his grasp. "Lincoln freed the slaves."

His answer was to lift her hand to his mouth, move his lips from the palm to the pulse in her wrist so that his breath seemed to reach through the skin to her blood till she was trembling.

"You know that I collect only things of beauty and value. These I cherish and protect. How could I do less for my wife?"

"I'm not a *thing*, Brandy. You can't keep me on velvet under a glass case. That's for Sleeping Beauties and—and corpses."

"You're so young, darling," he said with a maddeningly indulgent smile. "Look around at this group, at these older couples. One glance tells which women have been properly looked after. Like Beata Summerville. Sixty if she's a day, but she looks like a Greek goddess. Could she move with that grace and assurance if Mark didn't think her the most stunning woman in the world?"

Pondering the regal coronet of pure white hair showing above the back of Beata's seat, Tory had to admit there was a good deal of truth in what Brandy said. It was an education, watching the people who'd been married twenty, thirty, even forty years, and the one newlywed couple, Frieda and Harold Callahan, nicknamed the Gold Dust Twins because they had mops of red-gold curls worn the same length. In their early forties, they both taught biology at a private prep school in California, and had met after each lost a mate through long, ravaging illness. It was a testimony to human courage and resilience that Frieda and Hal had each sustained a dying loved one while working and caring for several children, emerging from their trials able to laugh and respond and love again.

"A lot of women have to *be* without a husband," Tory argued. "You can't call Morgan Scott dowdy or trammeled. Elspeth looks great when she wants to, and from what I hear, she protected and cosseted my uncle rather than the other way around." She cast a look over her shoulder at the eager zestful faces, smiled to hear Gaye Burns trying to show Mildred Halliday how to use a plant key to identify specimens. "I think all the single women are pretty great."

Brandy shrugged. "Interesting and spunky, yes. But some of the femininity of any woman living long without a man begins to atrophy except for huntresses like Morgan, who practice allure as a way of life."

"I like Morgan." For in spite of her sleek tailored black-pantherish beauty, Morgan's wry humor had several times smoothed over the irritations of travel in close quarters.

"My dear, so do I. But she's looking for a monied husband however much she chatters about the joys of earning her living as a free-lance photographer."

"That's no crime."

"Of course not. But she's not alone because she wants to be. I'll bet it was a great disappointment that there are no single men on this trip except Theron, who's a shade old and certainly not rich."

"I wish you wouldn't talk this way about people. It doesn't seem right to dissect their motives and personalities when we really don't know them that well."

Brandy gave her an amused stare. "You're an innocent, my sweetheart, but that's all right. I won't let you get into trouble." The running engine had muffled their voices. Now, as the last passenger boarded and Narciso shut the door, the bus roared and lurched onto the highway, making a sharp turn without spilling anyone into the aisle.

"Narciso's a good driver," commented Brandy. "But he takes that machismo stuff too seriously."

"So long as none of us do, it can't do any harm."

"All the same, Victoria, I'd suggest you stop saying *bueno* when he asks how you are. I wondered why he keeps cracking up about it and asked

Theron. *Bien* or *muy bien* is correct; *bueno* implies that you're good as in being good to eat."

Tory burst out laughing. "No wonder he went into convulsions. A little Spanish is a dangerous thing."

"It could be," agreed Brandy in an annoyingly patient tone.

Tory bit back a retort. She often felt callow and gauche around Brandy, but she didn't like it when he seemed to think so, too.

Fortunately Theron picked up the microphone and continued with the short lectures, which had already informed them that Yucatán possessed 429 species of birds, 285 of which bred there, the rest being winter residents, transients, and accidentals; 47 species of snakes including 7 poisonous ones, some with intriguing names such as Cuatro Narices (Four Noses) and the Yol Poc or Cola de Hueso (Tail of Bone).

"Yucatán has tertiary soil rather like that of Florida," Theron said. "The lowlands never have more than four inches of stony topsoil and the water is mostly underground, surfacing in *aguadas* and *cenotes*. Mayas still slash fields from the forests, use them two years, and then give the earth fifteen or so years to recover. As you can see from the crops here, the seed is tucked into almost any niche where it might take root and grow."

He answered a few questions and then sat down in front by Morgan Scott, who quickly had him plunged into some long explanation. Elspeth, in the seat ahead of Tory, looked both wistful and combative.

"Your aunt's thinking of some way to roast him," said Brandy. "Afraid I'll miss the fun. A client of mine's vacationing at Cancún and I need to discuss a few things with him."

Surprised, Tory started to ask why he hadn't mentioned it before, but she had made a vow to never, ever, intrude on her husband's business. This seemed a good moment to start training.

"Will you have enough time?" she asked.

"I'll make it enough. If Hastings requires more time, I'll rent a car at Akumal and drive up tomorrow while you hunt birds or enjoy the beach. I'd vote for the beach. It's fantastic." He gave her a slow smile that made her wish they were alone. "Just don't give any bronzed husky beachcombers a chance to kidnap you. There used to be pirates around here. The strain persists."

"Sounds like fun," said Tory, laughing. But she was a bit resentful that he expected all her attention when he was around so that she couldn't really mix with the group and make friends, and then saw no reason why he shouldn't leave her to spend the free day at Akumal alone.

It wasn't as alone as all that, though. She and Elspeth were up at 5:30 for the birdwalk and spotted a sacred *ceiba*, or kapok tree, adorned with Yucatán jays glinting bluish-green in the early sun. A cinnamon flower-piercer was demonstrating on the gorgeous yellow cascading blooms of a cassia tree. There were white-winged doves, black-cowled orioles, lineated woodpeckers, white-crowned parrots, glossy black great-tailed grackles, and what Elspeth assured Tory were variously Weid's crested flycatcher, yellow olive flycatcher, Yucatán flycatcher and the social flycatcher.

Theron happened to hear this last identification, studied the brown-backed, yellow-underbodied bird. "That's a great kiskadee," he said with mild positiveness. "They're both flycatchers, of course, and the boat-tailed flycatcher can be confused with either. But the social is smaller, has a short bill, and doesn't have the rufous wings and tails of our handsome fellow up there."

Scowling at him, Elspeth resorted to the bible of the tour, Peterson and Chalif's *A Field Guide to Mexican Birds*. Theron tactfully didn't wait to be proved right. Elspeth peered at the text and plates. She'd always been nearsighted, but had it gotten this much worse? Blushing, Elspeth shut the guide and grumbled, "Trust that odious man to know everything about a species called *Tyrannidae*."

"Why, Elspeth!" Tory was shocked. "Theron's not a tyrant. It's his job to tell us about the birds."

"He doesn't have to make a big thing of it every time he corrects me." Elspeth gave her crisp white curls a pugnacious shake. "Just because he belongs to the Wilson Ornithological Society, the Eastern Bird Banding Society, the Cornell Laboratory of Ornithology, Audubon, and I don't know what all, does that mean he's always right?"

"I'm sure he doesn't claim to be," Tory said in her most soothing tones.

What had gotten into Elspeth? She was usually the most generous-minded of people, though she could fly off the handle when someone didn't properly appreciate a choice book and had been known to refuse to sell to nonreading collectors who just wanted rare books to create a prestigious aura. It was a pity. Theron had at first hovered around Elspeth as much as any tour leader could with a group member, but he was beginning to almost sneak past her and his nice weathered face was beginning to wear a look of apprehension when she started to speak. Morgan Scott never contradicted him, but drank up his every word so that one could watch him relaxing, growing jaunty, and even strutting a bit.

It was elementary, but a glance at her aunt's woeful face convinced Tory that this wasn't the time to lecture on How to Lose a Man with Twenty-Five Words or Less. They rambled back to the resort, where incredibly white sand stretched down to the sparkling blue-green sea, so clear that one could see the white floor till coral and seaweed darkened it.

In the glass-walled round thatched restaurant, plates of fresh melon, papaya, and pineapple were already waiting. This was followed by scrambled eggs and bacon. The waiters wore red jackets, but the waitresses wore snowy *huipils* embroidered about the neck and swaying tiers that started at the hipline and reached to the floor. Large butterfly shaped scarlet or yellow ribbons perched at the nape of their necks beneath coiled black hair added to their flowerlike beauty, and Tory was content to linger over coffee till nearly everyone had drifted out and she had to decide how to spend this one special day.

Special because of the dazzling sea, and also because it might be her only free time on the tour. Free, meaning that there were no planned activities and, even more, that Brandy was gone. He'd rented a car and left before dawn, leaving a note to say he hoped Tory would miss him a lot but she shouldn't expect him back till late that night or possibly next morning.

Elspeth had looked at the note and chortled. "Reminds me of a friend who said she had a chimney that smoked, a rooster that crowed, and a cat that stayed out all night so what did she need with a husband."

Tory had grinned rather woodenly at that, but long before the early walk was over she'd found it pleasantly easy to move along with different members of the group, listen to Gaye Burns point out plants and flowers, Mildred Halliday imitate the melodious blackbird's "What cheerrr, what cheerr", and the white-eyed vireo's "Quick, gimme a raincheck, quick, gimme a raincheck." Beata Summerville was talking about a ruin just beyond the resort and Harold Callahan said that he and Frieda were going to find a substitute for the use of bird as a verb.

"Birding!" he snorted. "Sounds damned silly!" And Frieda's redhead bobbed in concurrence.

It was good to know people better, but though

she'd been invited to go with Elspeth and one group to Cobá's ruins and by another to go by boat to the island of Cozumel, Tory wanted to see what was in that unbelievable water, glide around the coral reefs, get down where the fishes were.

And there was a large diving-equipment place between the restaurant and the thatched bar down by the beach. As soon as she'd changed into her swimsuit and rubbed on sunscreen, she slipped on a terry robe and walked gingerly through the irradiating fine sand that crunched into her sandals with each step.

ALEXANDER GRANDE'S GREAT SWIM-DIVE SHOP said the sign in tutti-frutti letters shaped fancifully from octopuses, squid, fish, and shells. The owner must have a grande-great ego, Tory thought as she stepped into the cool shade.

When she could see after the glare, the *grande* shop was deserted. A counter stood in front of a rate schedule and a map of the coast and islands. Nets hung from the corners, obscuring various documents, clippings, and photos. A back room several times larger than the office had walls hung with masks, scuba tanks, flippers, and snorkels while some lethal-looking knives and spearguns were locked in a glass cabinet. From weighted belts, wet suits, life preservers, and other gear, Tory went back to examine the snorkeling things.

As if by magic a short muscular young man in purple glitter trunks and yellow jersey blazoned with ALEXANDER GRANDE appeared from behind a pile of tanks. He eyed Tory with such worry and appeal that she gave him an encouraging smile.

"I want to rent a snorkel and mask," she said slowly, hoping he might know English.

He shook his head.

"Snorkel?" repeated Tory.

Again the frantic signal of incomprehension.

Tory gestured from her face to the snorkeling equipment. "*Quiero* snor-kel?" she tried.

He stared at her hopelessly. Tory glanced around to see if some passerby might be able to interpret. There was no one in sight and when she turned back to the counter, her quarry had fled.

"Hello," she called. "*Buenos dias. Por favor. Señor*, please—"

But her entreaties produced no one. Tory groaned and gnawed her lip in frustration. If he didn't belong in the shop, why was he wearing that shirt? Snorkel was written up there on the rate chart, so apparently it was the same in Spanish. What was the matter anyway and *where* was Alexander the Great?

She patrolled the outside of the shop and asked at the restaurant and bar, but all she learned was that there really was an Alexander Grande, but he had gone off with the big boat and *Dios* alone knew when he'd be back. He had some helpers but—

But indeed!

Tory might have settled for a lazing swim if she hadn't been challenged, but now she was determined to snorkel. What a way to run a business!

If he wasn't going to attend to it, the resort should get a different man.

Aggravated past caution, Tory stalked as much as her sandals permitted back to the shop and pressed on a hand bell she hadn't noticed before.

It chirred. Nothing.

"*¡Hola!*" she called, trying to sound like a native. She rapped on the counter, too, but this time not even the yellow-jerseyed man appeared.

Tapping her foot, Tory turned to gaze out at the dancing sea, that beautiful translucent water, the dimly visible coral through which all manner of gorgeous fish were supposed to glide. Time was passing, she had only today. And Alexander Grande, drat him, was out with a big boat rather than bothering with forty-peso rentals of small gear. That was understandable, but why didn't he have someone to wait on customers?

Tory stared longingly at the water; all of a sudden her jaw snapped shut. She'd wait on herself. True, that was unorthodox, but so was leaving an open gear shop without an attendant. She'd write a note and pay later.

Just in case someone strolled in while she was selecting her equipment, Tory wrote the message first, giving the time and circumstances, her name and villa number. Securing the note with a big conch shell, she moved to the rear and studied the confusion of masks and snorkels.

She'd never snorkeled, but she understood the idea. You put the mouthpiece of the snorkeling tube in your mouth and breathed through it, while the mask allowed you to see under the water without getting brine in your eyes and nose.

She tried on masks till she found one that didn't swallow her upper lip or cramp about her nose, but she didn't want to taste-test a lot of snorkels, so she took one with a small mouthpiece and started to the beach.

Pinkish periwinkles grew in green-leafed clumps here and there on the shining sand. Most of the palms reared high to luxuriant fronds, but a few had succumbed to wind or accident and lay almost parallel to the ground, still thriving. It was an expensive resort and there were not many children playing in the sea or on the beach, but the people swimming or clustering at the thatched open bar and shelters were mostly Mexican. Probably most of them were tourists, but their presence made Tory feel less that she was at a tourist attraction.

An odd-shaped rock jutted out from shore. A tall white pole that might have been for flags or signals reared at the tip and beyond it was a small statuette. Tory promised herself to get a good look at the figure later on, while she was resting from her explorations, but it was hot and at the moment she could scarcely wait to leave sandals, robe, and sunglasses by a palm and wade into cooling, inviting waves that lapped gently about her ankles, then up her knees and waist as she progressed farther.

A pair of teenage boys were putting on their gear a little beyond her. She watched as they spat into their masks, then smeared this around with

sea water and rinsed out the masks. They gripped
the mouthpieces, angled the tubes through the
mask straps, and went down face-first to swim
lazily over the seaweed that now covered the bottom. They seemed to know what they were doing,
so Tory followed their example, but as she drifted
past the seaweed and glimpsed a huge round of
brain coral surrounded by a mass of yellow fish,
her delight was mingled with what one might call
a trickling certainty that all was not well with her
breathing arrangements. She was getting water in
her mouth.

As the amount increased, she involuntarily
breathed through her nose, didn't get air, felt the
instinctive dread of a land creature denied oxygen,
and must have opened her mouth, for water came
down her throat in a strangling gush.

Tory panicked, flailed the water, vainly trying
to touch bottom, fighting blindly at the mask and
snorkel. One foot struck something hard and sharp.
In spite of the pain, it was solid, and she tried to
find it again, to secure a footing and get her head
above water so she could breathe.

Then a strong grasp drew her to where her feet
brushed sand, helped her straighten and stand up-
right, while steellike fingers pulled off the stifling
mask.

For a moment, Tory gulped air, spewed water,
and scarcely noticed she was being supported by
an exceedingly firm arm.

"Better?" inquired an amused voice.

~❦ III ❦~

Tory gasped and nodded, blinking till she could gaze from a hard brown torso and throat up to a clefted chin, long mouth, and startling gray-green eyes. Her rescuer had thick wild auburn hair, streaked almost white in places from sun and water, and he wore what looked like a black obsidian twig around his throat on a thong. He resembled a pirate, and the slow grin that played at the corners of his mouth and crinkled the edges of his eyes added to that impression.

"Would you like to wash out that sea water with a nice rum and pineapple drink?" he asked.

Tory knew she looked like a drowned kitten. And he still had his arm around her; in fact, he was holding her a good deal closer than was necessary. Freeing herself with as much dignity as she could muster, she pushed her hair out of her face and tried to sound grateful, polite, and discouraging.

"Thanks very much. I—I guess I don't know how to use a snorkel. But I'm fine now. I don't care for a drink."

"Yes, you do. You're still shaking." He slipped his long brown hand about her wrist and moved her irresistibly along. "After you're warmed up and are over your scare, I'll show you how to use this gear."

"Really, I can't!" Tory protested.

This man was damnably attractive—knew it, too—but he mustn't think her a beach pickup. Besides, what would Brandy say? She had a flash of conviction that he'd rather have her drown than loll about sipping rum with this sea-eyed man whose lean muscular body and manner was charged with male vitality.

He cocked his head at her. "Would you rather be arrested for theft?"

"Theft?" she echoed.

"Yes, indeed." He flourished the mask and snorkel he was carrying for her. "You snitched these out of my swim shop."

"I—I did not," she spluttered, trying to pull free. "I tried and tried to find someone and finally left a note."

"Notes," he said blandly, "have a way of blowing off in the sea breeze."

"I weighted it down with a shell that weighed at least three pounds."

He shook his head sadly. "Too bad they still operate on the Napoleonic Code down here. Guilty till proven innocent."

She planted her feet in the sand, the cut on her foot smarting at the abrasiveness. He stopped, too, but kept a relaxedly secure grip on her. "You!" she accused. "Are *you* this Alexander Grande?"

His eyes danced like the play of sun on water. She'd never met such an overwhelming man and it didn't help much to tell herself it was all bronze and muscles. He was physical all right, but he radiated a force, a controlled energy that emphasized even more what came across as an untamed, even wild spirit.

"My friends call me Zan." He grinned.

Ridiculous to ask a man like this why he didn't mind the store, but . . . wasn't he trying to blackmail her? "*Mr.* Grande," she said with frost, "when a shop like yours is the only one of its kind, it has an obligation to serve customers."

"If I'd known you were coming, I'd have been there," he said in mock contrition.

She tried, with predictable lack of success, to stamp her foot in the knee-deep water. "That's not the point."

"Gregorio was there. If you'd been a man, he'd have helped you."

"If I'd been a man!" Tory couldn't believe her ears. "You mean you go off and leave things to a purple-glitter addict who won't wait on women?"

"He's scared of *gringas*. One tried to take him back to Rhode Island with her. Since then the sight of an unescorted *norteamericana* sends him into quakes."

"If that's so, you can scarcely blame *gringas* for taking what they need and I think you're darned lucky I left a note."

"And *you're* lucky I got back in time to see you floundering around." There was no disputing that, and Tory kept still. "Let's have that drink," he coaxed. "You *do* need it. And then to make up for my shortcomings as an entrepreneur, I'll give you a private intensive course in snorkeling. Hundred-dollar value and cheap at the price."

"I begin to understand the Grande," she murmured. "Bet it's not even your real name."

"I knew it the moment I saw you choking on your snorkel. A woman of discernment as well as beauty. My real name is Ericson, but I needed something to appeal to the local trade."

"From the way you run your shop, I'd never have thought you worried about any kind of trade."

He gestured as if stabbed. "I swear you do me wrong. But taking the big boat out pays well."

"And it's more fun than hanging around the counter."

"I knew you were discerning." He drew her toward the shore. She winced as sand worked into the cut place on her foot. "What's wrong?" he asked.

She raised her foot from the water and a flow of red quickly showed on the instep. "You must have done it on the coral," he said, real concern in his voice. "Coral infections are the very devil."

"It's not much of a cut."

"I've seen smaller cause problems that took months to heal." Before she guessed what was happening, he swept her up in his arms, strode through the water.

"I can walk," she protested.

"You're not getting more junk in that gash. I've got some good antiseptic and bandage."

He was probably exaggerating the septicity of the coral, but it *was* a relief not to get sand gritted in the cut each time she took a step. Besides, it was futile to argue. He bore her along like a buccaneer appropriating his spoils and his eyes probed hers, so piercingly bright and close that she shut her own as if the sun were blinding her.

Not being able to see simply made her more aware of the deep steady sound of his heart, the strength of the hard arms holding her so effortlessly. She couldn't imagine Brandy carrying her like this; he might put his arm around her and help her limp. But after all, she defended quickly, Brandy was *civilized*. Not a savage who relied on brawn and hoked-up pizzazz.

She was being lowered to a seat. Alexander Zan Ericson Grande seemed reluctant to let go of her, but he was back in a moment with a bottle, a tube of medicine, gauze, scissors, and elastic bandage.

"Yell if you want," he invited, opening the bottle of violent green. He took her foot and doused it with liquid stinging fire.

Tory gasped, held her breath, and blinked back tears of shock. Her rescuer gave her leg a sympathetic pat. "Good girl. The salve won't hurt.

And once you're all bandaged, a little rum will make you good as new."

"Will this keep me out of the water?" she asked, frowning, as he secured the gauze with a loop of broad elastic bandage.

"How long will you be here?"

"Just today."

"We-e-ell, I suppose I can loan you a wet-suit boot. But," he decreed, "there's no way you can go out without me to make sure you don't drown and lose my valuable property."

He *had* been kind. Truth to tell, Tory, after her frightening experience, wasn't so keen on snorkeling alone. Not till she learned how to breathe. So she laughed and surrendered.

Sipping pineapple juice with a touch of rum, Tory learned that Zan, as she soon caught herself calling him, was from Montana, but his parents had always vacationed on the Caribbean beach and, by the time he was in his teens, he spent his summers there, eager for the day he could live there year round.

"That was ten years ago," he said growing serious. "I've had a great time and I love this sea. But I've never given up my U.S. citizenship and the past year or two I've been thinking it was time I found someplace in the States where I could run a business—California, Florida, maybe even Padre Island off the Texas coast—and just vacation here or sign on special expeditions." He grinned at her, but those changing gray-green eyes were intent. "Do you like water, Tory?"

"There are lakes around Dallas, but most of my swimming's been in the YWCA pool."

"You can't help where you were raised," he said. "But tame water, that's not for me. I like to feel the ocean's power coming in on the waves, feel that connection to the deepest greatest world of all, the one we know the least about but where all life came from."

Yes. He'd love the wild waters, the surging waves and limitless force. Tory, close as she'd been to drowning, couldn't share his enthusiasm, not just then. A sort of inner trembling began in her and she didn't know if it was a physical reaction from her fright or the impact of Zan's closeness, the smiling touch of those eyes, which never seemed to be the same color for more than seconds.

This was no way for an engaged person to be feeling! Breaking the moment of silent intimacy, Tory learned that Zan had dived with Jacques Cousteau and was a member of CEDAM, Club de Exploraciones y Deportes Acuáticos de México, or the Club of Explorations and Water Sports.

"Foreign divers were pillaging sunken galleons, sacred wells, and underground river sites," Zan explained. "Apart from promoting water sports, CEDAM was founded to locate and salvage under-water archaeological and historical treasures and explore for oil and mineral wealth while working with the related ministries of the Mexican government. It's done important work and not a bit too soon. Theft and resale of treasures and artifacts is big business in Mexico. It'd make you sick to see the way looters dynamite and hack at a site to get pieces they can smuggle out and sell at tremendous profits."

Would Brandy buy objects obtained in such a way? Horrified that she couldn't immediately reject such a thought, Tory remembered how he'd lingered in the caverns, absorbed in the jaguar and mound of sacred figures, how he'd seemed to feel it was a waste for them to be there.

She couldn't reflect on that long, though, for Zan was telling how CEDAM had fought a legal battle to salvage from the *Matanceros,* a Spanish merchant ship wrecked near here in the first part of the eighteenth century.

"A foreigner had been diving there and felt he had first claim. CEDAM won the case and then invited the guy to dive with them and keep half the finds."

"And what was found?" Tory asked, entranced with the reality of sunken galleons and buried treasure.

Zan shrugged. "Four ship cannon, semiprecious stones, jewelry, pewter, silver spoons, needles, thimbles, three thousand crosses, and lots more of the same kind of articles. No troves of gold, though a head curator of the Smithsonian appraised the salvage and said that in quantity and diversity of objects, this was the richest shipwreck explored to date." He gazed out to sea and his mouth hardened. "It's rumored, though, that a foreigner buried several chests of loot from the *Matanceros* in hopes of one day getting it out of the country. Maybe he's already succeeded." Pointing toward the figure out of the rocks that Tory had noticed earlier, Zan said affectionately, "There's the real treasure of the *Matanceros,* to my mind."

"What is it?"

"Come and see." He glanced at her foot, his gaze lingering an admiring moment on legs that Tory knew were shapely. "Can you walk?"

"Of course I can." She evaded his outstretched hand and put down her empty glass, but she bit her lip when she put her weight on the injured, now stiffening foot.

Zan saw. Brooking no resistance, he slipped his arm under hers. "Don't tussle," he warned. "I'd like an excuse to carry you again."

"Shouldn't you be at your shop?"

"Gregorio's there." Zan chuckled. "I'll have to rescue him if we notice any *gringas* going in."

"You no doubt enjoy such rescues."

"It all depends." His gaze sent strange tumultuous currents racing through her. She tore her eyes away, concentrated on the metal figure at the end of the rock.

Her sandals slipped on the stone, and Zan's steadying if annoyingly masterful arm kept her from several falls by the time they reached the jutting low promontory.

"Close your eyes," Zan said.

Tory did, allowed him to guide and turn her around. "Now, Tory."

She looked down at a sweet grave face, a crowned slender madonna outlined with jagged rays, weathered bronzish green. Blessing those who were at sea, she was quite the loveliest image Tory had ever seen.

"You're right," she told Zan. "She is the real treasure of the wreck."

"There are other things up in the museum by the office. Why don't we go up and have a look? Then we could have a light lunch and wait for the sun to start down a little before you have that private lesson."

"Oh, I can't take that much of your time."

"You're not. You're sharing. Giving me your time." His hand touched the side of her cheek, lightly, yet she felt again that dizzying, sweetly irresistible male force of his, different from anything she'd ever experienced.

Taking her assent for granted, he smiled, bowed to the small madonna, and helped Tory back across the slippery rocks. Shouting a good-natured admonition through the shop door at the sheepish Gregorio, Zan kept his hand under Tory's arm as they strolled up the palm-bordered lane to the office. Zan took a few minutes to explain the magnificent statuary on a pedestal in front of the resort, a conquistador wearing Indian garb, an Indian woman, and two children, one a little girl playing with a steel helm almost as big as she was. Tory thought it a charmingly intimate yet heroic sculpture.

"The Spaniard is Gonzalo de Guerrero, whose

caravel was shipwrecked near Jamaica. He drifted to this shore with twelve companions, but five of them were sacrificed and ritually devoured by the Mayans. Guerrero may have been too skinny. However that was, after some period of slavery he served a northern Maya lord who was so impressed by his courage and ability that he married his own daughter to him. Later, when he was asked to rejoin the Spaniards, Guerrero refused out of love for his family. His children were the first mestizos born in this country, though now, of course, bloods have become very mixed."

"It's good to hear about a man who didn't abandon his native family," Tory said.

Zan nodded. "Yucatán was discovered by the Spanish in 1511, but the Maya were never completely subdued. Though many were serf laborers, a long kind of guerrilla war broke out against the whites and mestizos in 1848, and kept flaring up till about 1900, when the central government finally conquered the Cruzob, Mayas who were united by a cult of the Talking Cross. Some of them fled into the wilds of Quintana Roo, the state where you are. And believe me, it's still pretty wild."

They wandered to the sparkling white museum, where a swarthy man who knew Zan joked with him as he paid admission. Zan chatted for a while as Tory meandered along the glass cases, peering at coins, utensils, jewelry, all kinds of relics from the ship, and other finds from the region. Zan joined her after a while and, after she had looked at everything, said that he was famished.

Because of their clothing, they ate on the terrace of the restaurant, having Zan's recommended conch meat with lime juice, and crystal compotes of chilled juicy mangoes, strawberries, bananas, and pineapple.

Three handsome men with guitars, wearing exquisitely worked white *guayaberas,* the dress shirts that doubled for jackets, greeted Zan and bowed gallantly as he introduced them to Tory.

"They want to sing for you," Zan said.

"I don't know anything but 'La Paloma' and 'Cielito Lindo.' "

"Texas!" said Zan. "We can do better than that."

He spoke to the musicians, who nodded, smiled admiringly at Tory, and began to harmonize with happy-sad music that had to be of love. Then, at a suggestion from Zan, they moved into a song so hauntingly beautiful that even though she couldn't understand the words, Tory felt tears fill her eyes.

"What is this song?" she asked.

" 'La Peregrina.' It was written for another *norteamericana* who came here and fell in love with the Maya who was then governor of Yucatán, Felipe Carrillo Puerto. He was shot to death at the instigation of wealthy landowners, but La Peregrina, the traveler, stayed in Mexico."

Violence and beauty and love and death. There seemed to be a lot of all of them in the history of this land. After the musicians had joined them for a drink, paying Tory extravagant compliments in halting English but unmistakable looks, they wandered to another table, and Zan and Tory went over to his shop, where he found a rubberized boot to fit snugly above the ankle.

"Now for your lesson," he said. Something in his eyes made Tory sure he was talking about more than how to use a snorkel.

~IV~

The first thing Zan did was show her how to fit the mouthpiece *under* her lips, not over them. It made a tremendous difference, though her jaws soon ached from keeping a nervously tight grip on the rubber.

"Don't scrape on the coral," warned Zan. "And watch out for sea urchins. They can really make you smart if you blunder into them." He grinned. "Hey, you don't have to bite the mouthpiece to death. Relax and come with me."

He launched forward and she followed, over the seaweed and into the cliffs and gardens of a new world. Boulders and coral reefs formed canyons through which fantastic fish glided. There were forests of water plants, some straight like cucumbers, others like miniature trees, and great fanlike leaves that swayed gently with a life of their own. A little black fish darted out from a mass of plants and nipped Tory's knee. Apparently he was defending eggs, for he lost interest in her once she had moved past his territory.

The coral made exquisitely sculptured castles

and masses. There were many kinds of it, and Tory found the waterscape, the plants and reefs, almost as fascinating as the fish. Sun rays filtered in strange shimmering prisms and refractions through the translucent water down to the white sand of the bottom. Completely enchanted, Tory could have drifted lazily for hours, swimming only to avoid being washed by the current into the rocks or coral, but her jaws were hurting from the mouthpiece.

Zan had been roaming near her. As if he could read signs of her flagging, he arced gracefully past, motioning, stepped on a pile of rock and held her so that she could raise her head and breathe without the snorkel for a while.

"Feel good?" He laughed as she spluttered and worked her jaws. "Isn't it great down there?"

"Marvelous! It's another world. The way the plants swayed in the current—that was just like trees or flowers bending in the wind on earth."

He nodded, eyes glowing at her pleasure. "Welcome to my world, Tory."

Before she could guess his intention, he gave her a kiss that began light, gay, and then changed, his lips moving on hers, hungry, insistent, making her feel almost as swept away and helpless as she had when she'd almost drowned.

For a moment, involuntarily, her arms tightened around him. He gave a soft husky laugh, and she felt as if she had absolutely no defenses against him, no resistance.

This wouldn't do! She scarcely knew him, he

probably did this with all the *turistas,* and besides, she was in love with Brandy! Jerking her head away as far as she could, which wasn't far because he had a firm grip on her, Tory glared.

"You—you took advantage!"

"Why not?"

"Because—because you ought to be ashamed of yourself! Coaxing people out here and—"

"Ninety-nine percent of my clients will get from me only professional handling." He wasn't the slightest bit ashamed. "But that other percent better look out!"

He bent his head again, but Tory averted her face, their snorkels jutting from behind their mask straps got tangled, and by the time Zan got them unmuddled Tory was giggling wildly.

"No romance in your soul, wench." Sighing, Zan handed her the snorkel. "No sense of this fateful moment!"

"One that must happen every time you lure an unwary female out over her head!"

He cocked a sun-streaked but still dark eyebrow. "So you're over your head? I'm encouraged!"

"Don't be! My fiancé gets back tonight, tomorrow's fully scheduled, and we leave next morning."

"Woe upon woe," he lamented. "And worst woe of all, did you breathe that awful word 'fiancé'?"

"No doubt it sounds awful to you," she said coldly. "But some men, mature men, don't mind committing themselves."

"Mature," pondered Zan. "That means stodgy.

Bet he's a plump middle-aged stockbroker who's losing his hair."

Tory gave a yelp of wordless outrage, then composed herself as best she could while depending on this obnoxious man to keep her head above water. "Brandy's exceedingly handsome and charming. He's a collector and dealer in art objects and—"

"He decided to add you to his collection of beautiful things."

"You—you have absolutely no right to say that!"

"But it's true, isn't it?" thrust Zan.

Tory couldn't answer. Unwilling memories of Brandy's possessiveness flashed through her mind; but that was just his way of showing love, surely. Brandy couldn't marry a woman he took no pride in. Sometimes it was difficult to live up to his standards, but Tory had taken that as a challenge she should try to meet. Zan's remarks made her wonder—and wondering made her feel treacherous. She stared at Zan in mute defiance.

"Think about it," he advised. "What's your bunch doing tomorrow?"

"Going to Tulum after the six-o'clock birdwalk and breakfast. We'll carry box lunches and stop at some lagoon on the way back."

"That'll be Xel Ha. It's got wonderful underwater caverns and good fish. You'll need your snorkel."

"Maybe I can rent one there."

Zan chuckled. "No, you can't, Tory. I'm the only game in town."

"A shame you don't have some competition."

His hand caressed her shoulder. "Now who could compete with me?"

"Someone who tended shop," she retorted. "Zan, we have to get back. Your place is probably full of unfortunate women that Gregorio's hiding from."

"Maybe they'll be enterprising like you and take what they want. Don't apologize," he teased as she started to protest. "I honor you for it. People should go after what they need."

"Not when it belongs to somebody else."

"That didn't keep you from helping yourself to my equipment."

"Which you should have been looking after!"

"Call it a tie," he suggested. "But people aren't objects, Tory. They don't belong *to* anyone, though they may belong *with* them."

He'd certainly never belong to anyone and she'd bet he wouldn't be with anyone very long, either. One might as well dream of netting the wind, caging the waves, capturing the sunlight.

"No doubt you've explained this to many ladies who thought you were with them when you were way ahead," she mocked.

The warmth left his eyes and the reckless grin faded. "I guess you're right," he said. "It's time we went back."

His hands were impersonal as he helped her adjust mask and snorkel, launch into that magic world just beneath the blue-green surface.

Coral ramparts were as magnificent as before; blue and yellow and shimmering rainbow-colored fish moved through grottoes and undulating tendrils and leaves. Tory had to admire all she saw, but part of the miracle of the journey out was Zan's sharing his sea with her.

He wasn't, now. He was leading, escorting. Tory followed him into the shallows, got to her feet, and felt like collapsing back into the waves.

"I feel so *heavy*," she blurted at Zan's questioning look.

"Yes, you're back with gravity again, a body that has weight." He didn't offer to help her, though she felt exhausted, as if she weighed a ton and each step required tremendous effort. "You'll be fine as soon as your body adjusts to the realities of life onshore."

Tory took his advice. In a few minutes she felt normal again and walked with Zan to where their sandals and her robe were. "I don't see why our ancestors ever left the water," she grumbled.

"Probably got stranded in tide pools till their lungs got able to handle air." Zan thawed a little. "Wouldn't it be neat to be an amphibian and have it both ways?"

"I can't say that I've ever longed to be a turtle or toad." Tory laughed. "But it would be great to be able to breathe underwater just as it'd be fun to fly like a bird."

"Sea and air are a lot alike," said Zan. "Currents and unexpected drops and eddies, elemental force that can buoy or smash you, depending on how you meet it."

Like love? Quelling the unbidden thought, Tory

worked off the tight-fitting rubber boot. Zan examined the bandage. "A tad damp," he said. "Let me put on a fresh one."

"Oh, that's so much trouble—"

"You don't know what trouble is till you get a coral infection." He took her boot, mask, and snorkel, but didn't help her to her feet. "I've known them to fester around for months. Your collector fiancé wouldn't like that."

He wouldn't. And he was going to be angry when he learned she'd gone out alone. Tory sighed, hoping she wouldn't have to confess all her stupidities, and tried not to limp as she went with Zan to his shop.

He applied the new bandage with practiced skill, much as he might have treated Gregorio, accepted Tory's pesos as if they were too unimportant to argue about, and then picked up something from the counter.

"Keep this to remember Akumal," he said. "Maybe she'll help you next time you're in deep waters."

Tory gazed down at a small bronze replica of the *Matanceros* madonna fitted to a chain. "Why, she's lovely, Zan. But you shouldn't give her to me."

"Why not?"

"You must have bought her at the museum. Before I—you—"

"Before I knew you were on a collector's shelf?" he finished grimly. "True. But whatever you think, Tory, I want you to have the little sea guardian."

There was nothing to do but keep it. Tory thanked him, finding his gaze very hard to meet. Why did he look so stern, almost hurt? It was all a game to him, an entertainment. For all she knew he got a special discount on madonnas and gave them away by the gross.

"Thanks, Zan," she said, trying for lightness. "It was a *grande* afternoon."

A tall tanned girl with blond hair strolled in, most of her sensuously bared by a black bikini. Zan said briskly to Tory, "Enjoy yourself," and turned to his new customer.

Tory stepped outside and told herself that stinging in her eyes came from sea salt. Why should she be disappointed that he hadn't asked to see her again? It was impossible. She was going to marry Brandy. The magnetism flowing between Zan and her was one of those brief tempestuous vacation attractions, unexpected and wild as a tropical storm, nothing that could last.

Yet when she reached her villa and let herself into the shade, she felt a deep sense of loss.

Would she never see him again? The sharp-edged rays haloing the madonna bit into her palm. She sat down and gazed at the small tranquil figure for a long long time.

The straggling return of other tour members from their various expeditions was heralded by shouts and laughter from surrounding villas. Elspeth came in, touting the splendors of Cobá and the relief of getting away from that overbearing Theron, who apparently was still out in the brush somewhere with Morgan Scott and the Summervilles. Halfway through a glass of the potable water stored in a glass jug hung so it could be easily tilted, Elspeth noticed Tory's foot.

"Heavens, child! What's happened to your foot?"

Tory explained as tersely as she could, but Elspeth, after all, had known her through the teen years when Tory had defended every shred of personal information as if it were a garment she had clutched about her.

"So you were rescued by a young buccaneer and you've taken quite a fancy to him." Elspeth's hazel eyes were benign. "No harm in that, dear. Gather ye snorkelers while ye may."

"I can't! I'm engaged!"

"Well, if that's the only reason, you'd better unengage!" said her aunt, sniffing. "Marriage is, or should be, for keeps. Be mighty sure before you get into it."

Tory gave a sniff of her own. "I suppose that even after I'm married I'll still notice attractive, appealing men."

"You'd better notice them very quietly with Brandon for a husband." Aunt and niece scowled at each other for a moment, then burst into laughter and a mutual hug. "The thing is," said Elspeth, sobering, "that you can admire other men and enjoy their company, but if you still wouldn't rather be with the man you chose, if he isn't worth passing up the others, then maybe you picked the wrong man. I'd hate for you to do that, honey."

Tory couldn't imagine Zan ever being eclipsed, even for a moment, by another man. He and Brandy were so different that there was no way to compare them. In fact, there was no way to compare Zan with anyone Tory had ever known. He was raffish and wild and irresponsible. Look at the way he ran—or didn't run—his business! She wished Brandy would get back and help banish him from her mind.

"Speaking of choices," Tory said, deciding to lecture her aunt for a change. "The way you've been acting doesn't leave poor Theron with much choice between you and Morgan. You were getting along so well at first, but lately you've argued with him at every turn. He's a sweet man, but you can't expect him to enjoy being flatly contradicted all the time."

Elspeth flushed. Her skin was incredibly fresh and youthful-looking, striking with her soft white hair. "I won't kowtow to him," she said. "And I won't shove people aside to get to him, either. Haven't you noticed how Morgan just seems to surround him? And," she added bitterly, "he seems content enough to be surrounded."

So that was it! But sympathy wasn't what Elspeth needed. "You can't blame him for that, the way you've been acting. You've been a real shrew, darling."

"But when he misidentifies—"

"Elspeth, love," chided Tory, "he hasn't been

wrong yet on a positive identification. If you'll remember back, you'll realize that every time you've argued, you've been wrong or the sighting was so questionable that no one was really sure."

Hazel eyes widening, Elspeth reflected on that. A deep mortified flush swept from her neck to her hair. "As bad as that? I feel like going home."

"No, you don't!" Tory flung her arms around her aunt and gave her a squeeze. "The tour's still young. Just be yourself, and when Theron sees he's not going to get his head bit off, he'll come around."

"Morgan won't let him," Elspeth said gloomily. She lifted her chin and managed a smile. "Well, anyway, I can enjoy the tour. I've already got eighty-nine species listed and fifty are firsts for my life list. Isn't Brandy back?"

"He said he might be late or even come back tomorrow."

"Must be a very important client."

"I suppose so. Anyway, he has a car and our itinerary. He can always catch up."

But he didn't come by the time the group began collecting for dinner. The spot next to Tory, which everyone assumed to be his, stayed vacant, and on her other side Elspeth chatted away with Beata Summerville. Across the long table, Frieda and Hal were still trying to come up with a better verb than "birding."

A bit glumly Tory ate her way through delectable turtle soup, broiled lobster, fried bananas, and crunchy coconut ice cream, all so good that her spirits were lifting from sheer gustatory satisfaction, when Zan came in. He was with the lissome blonde who'd come into the shop as Tory was leaving, and from the way they were laughing and watching each other, they had very quickly gotten acquainted.

They took a table for two at the window. As if drawn by Tory's eyes, Zan glanced toward her. From the way his eyebrow climbed, he saw and understood the empty seat by her. He gave her a polite nod and turned back to his companion.

Pain curled through Tory like a sly razor that didn't hurt till the bleeding started. If he had to come flaunting his conquests, why, at least, couldn't Brandy have been here?

And why, *why* did she ache like this over an almost stranger?

~V~

Tulum's three-sided ancient walls were crumbling about the city, but its fourth barrier, limestone cliffs above the pounding, ever-breaking sea, was as effective as ever. The native guide acquired at the site informed them that Tulum had been founded by the Mayas between A.D. 300 and 500 and exposed to Toltec influence about 900 years later. Gonzalo de Guerrero had been commander-in-chief here and perhaps had built the walls as a defense against his own invading Spanish countrymen.

Tulum was sacred to the setting sun, worshiped as the diving god, and some experts believed that his trapezoidal tail symbolized the rattlesnake as might the similarly shaped cornices and certain buildings.

Pointing out the bones of an archaeologist, whose pursuits had evidently not been appreciated, where he had been plastered into a wall, the guide went off to enlighten a newly arrived busload of Germans. Theron announced a half-hour period to ramble, after which they would go birding around the mangrove forest.

"Birding," muttered Hal Callahan. "To bird. Sounds crazy. There has to be a better word."

Laughing for the first time that day—for Brandy was still missing and she was irrationally haunted by the memory of Zan's unruly head bent attentively toward the sleek blonde—Tory climbed with hardier souls up the main structure and walked the narrow ledge around to the side that looked down on the crashing white surf, the limitless sea beyond. She sat there, mesmerized by the waves, till Theron's whistle summoned the group.

Dodging through the German group and another that seemed predominantly French, Tory helped form the rear guard of Theron's little column as they followed a road running through a parklike stretch of trees and came to more ruins, these largely overgrown with vines and trees. Following a trail down past powdering limestone walls, they entered a low dense hollow where the air was so humid and thick and strong-scented that one could almost touch it.

Theron and the Bowdries had glimpsed something in the mangroves, and Tory dutifully brought up her binoculars, but she only saw a flitting shape back in the leaves.

At that moment she couldn't have worked up much excitement over a resplendent quetzal. She had forgotten her hat. Her head throbbed. The cut on her foot hurt. She felt as if she could scarcely extract any oxygen from the heavy air.

"I'm going back to the bus," she muttered to Elspeth.

"Oh, dear!" The constant menace of Aztec two-step hung over everybody, though Theron had booked them into the best and cleanest hotels and restaurants. Elspeth caught Tory's hand. "Not—?"

"I don't think so. May have got a little too much sun yesterday." And too much, or not enough, Alexander Grande.

"Shall I come with you?" her aunt said, worried.

"Gracious, no! But I wouldn't stay in this oven another ten minutes to see all the birds in Yucatán." Laughing as she whispered this last heresy, Tory gave her aunt a reassuring pat on the shoulder and continued along the path circling back beneath the principal ruins to the parking lot.

It was a relief to be moving, but this was the hottest part of the day. Trees and plants fairly seemed to steam. Tory experienced her body as an unwieldy lethargic weight that she had increasing difficulty in steering along the rough stony trail. But she could see the parking lot ahead, the equivalent of a block beyond the thatched shed she was approaching. As she drew even with the shed, her foot slipped on a loose rock.

Down she went, bruising her rear and her dignity, scraping the hand she threw back to break the fall. Two boys who were weaving hats from palm fronds stared at her with big dark eyes, but a smaller girl dissolved into giggles. Tory knew she looked comic even without the tangle of camera and binoculars around her neck.

Gingerly making sure she hadn't broken anything, she got shakily up on one knee, was seized by the elbows, and hauled to her feet.

"What are you doing without a hat?" demanded Zan. He produced a big white handkerchief and wiped off her face and cut hand as if she'd been a troublesome child. "I'd thought that at least on dry land you could take care of yourself."

"What—what are you doing here?" she gasped.

"I've joined the tour."

"You?"

"Sure. I've always wanted to know about birds. This is my chance."

"You can't just barge in like this!"

"Want to bet?" He examined the green hats, selected one, tried it on Tory, and nodded, giving one of the boys some pesos. "I talked it over last night with Theron Powers. He's delighted to have me, especially since we're going to Palenque, where I know the Lacandon chief and can arrange for some really unusual sidetrips for the hardy souls who want them." He eyed her critically. "I don't think you'd survive."

"Thank you very much," said Tory, seething. She took off the hat and thrust it into his hands. "You—you're more *macho* than any Latin ever thought about being. I don't have to prove a thing to you!"

"Good. Wear the hat then like a sensible person and let's find something to drink."

She was indeed thirsty and knew she needed something on her head, which felt as if overheated blood was swelling the veins and threatening to split her skull. Zan peered at her, swore in dismay, and got her under the shelter, making her sit on a bench where a pile of hats was building.

"Stay here," he ordered. "I'll get you a drink. If you think you're going to faint, put your head between your knees."

Tory gave him a weak glare, but she had no inclination to rise. He was back in a few minutes with a cold sarsaparilla and dampened handkerchief.

"Sip it easy," he advised. He cooled her face and throat with the cloth, finished by holding it on her wrists. Funny how such a small thing could make one feel so much better.

"Thanks," said Tory shamefacedly. "You really have been very kind."

He grinned impudently. "I've got reasons."

She had a sudden dreadful thought. "The pretty woman you were with last night—is she coming on the tour?"

"Lauren? She doesn't care about birds. She's been coming down with her family for years. I taught her to swim and dive and handle a boat."

"Practically a sister!"

Zan chuckled. "I wouldn't say that. Each year the kid improves considerably. But she's going to play sun goddess like crazy the next few weeks. Blond hair, as you've noticed, is scarce down here."

Voices sounded. "Here come your buddies," said Zan. "How come your fiancé let you come ahead by yourself?"

"He must still be in Cancún."

"Great!" Zan beamed. "Then I can sit with you."

"I suppose so. How'd you get over here?"

"Oh, it took me a while to set my shop in order this morning, but I caught a ride with a French tour bus. Even brought snorkeling gear for the crowd to use at Xel Ha."

"I can't keep you from coming on the tour if Mr. Powers agreed," said Tory severely. "I can only hope that today will convince you that you're really not all this interested in birds."

"But I am." His eyes sparkled, though he managed to sound plaintive.

"And—and you surely know that my fiancé won't like it if you . . ." Her voice trailed off. His eyes gleamed brighter.

"If I hang around you?" he supplied. "Thus far his presence certainly hasn't been a problem. But never fear. When and if the lucky Brandon appears I'll pay strict attention to bird book and binoculars." He eyed her quizzically. "From what Theron says, your intended is a mite old and picky for you."

"You had the nerve to go asking a lot of questions?"

"Not a *lot*. A few. I just happened to remark that I'd heard of the tour through a young lady who'd—shall we say *patronized* my shop—and inquired if her fiancé had returned."

"Ohhh! You're incredible!"

"Think of what I could have said. That you

helped yourself to my equipment, almost drowned and— By the way, how's your foot?"

"Fine," she lied.

"I brought the salve and gauze. After we snorkel at Xel Ha, I'll change the bandage."

"Alexander Ericson, you cannot just push in and act like my keeper!"

"You'd rather get a nasty lingering coral infection that'll last long after my odious memory has faded?"

That would be impossible. She'd never forget him. "Could you let me buy the salve, please?"

He sighed. "I suppose I can't continue cuddling your foot once your humorless Brandon materializes."

The group was scattered about them now, some buying hats and seed-and-berry necklaces, others making for the cold-drink box, some getting gratefully on the bus. Narciso always started the motor and air-conditioning ten or fifteen minutes before the bus was needed so that it'd be cool.

Tory introduced Zan to an exceedingly curious Elspeth, and they got on the bus while he lingered to joke with Narciso, whom he obviously knew. Narciso's eyes had been even more admiring when he handed Tory up the steps. Apparently it was considered a triumph to catch Zan's attention.

"So!" accused Elspeth from the seat behind Tory. "I thought there was more than you admitted to your day on the beach. And he's joining the tour? Fantastic!"

"Wretched," growled Tory. "How even he can

dream of leaving a business in charge of a man who flees at sight of *gringas* is beyond me. Total lack of responsibility."

Elspeth laughed as she watched Zan and Narciso chatting gaily. "Well, dear, he seems to have considerable initiative. That young man will always earn a living, but he'll have fun doing it."

The bus filled amid glowing descriptions of masked tityras, green-breasted mango hummingbirds, rufous-browed peppershrikes and ferruginous pygmy owls. Zan got in last.

"See how craftily I'm protecting your reputation?" Zan slid in beside Tory with a virtuous air. "No other place for me to sit but here, unless I'm antisocial and go to the back."

"Which you'll have to do when Brandy turns up," she reminded him sharply.

"That's later. This is now." He gave her a lazy smile. Her heart turned over. The weakness she'd felt in the mangrove heat was nothing to the way her bones now treacherously seemed to melt.

Absolute madness! Zan was a fearsomely attractive male with the added reflected glamour of the sea, the paradisiacally beautiful coast. He was a wild, crazy, out-of-place moment. Brandy was her future, the man who belonged to real life. He'd rejoin the tour tonight and this episode with Zan would fade into the past.

She had to remember that.

The palm-bordered lagoon shone like sapphire, and though its waters were not so astoundingly clear as the sea, there was no coral and Tory could perch safely on the great piles of underwater boulders. Zan was helping first-time snorkelers, but when everyone was managing satisfactorily, he took Tory under the rope into the deep water and showed her the caverns, then led her to rest on a sort of natural bridge that was only a few inches underwater.

She had been getting chilled and the sun felt good. She closed her eyes and enjoyed it, conscious that Zan was watching her, warmed, too, by his gaze.

"So how do you like the country?" he asked. "Pretty as the postcards?"

She laughed, opening her eyes to the deep blue of the lagoon, swaying palms, a small island. It was worth delving into her small supply of Spanish. *"Encantadora."* she said.

"So are you." Though he didn't touch her, his nearness had an electrical impact. For once he wasn't smiling. "Come on," she said hastily. "Theron's beckoning his flock."

Tory, like the others, had worn her swimsuit under regular clothes, but hadn't wanted to struggle them on so she had dripped on the sand a few minutes and then used the towel to protect the seat.

This strategy had been followed by everyone except Beata, who had a wraparound skirt so Tory felt no self-consciousness about getting off the bus.

Till she saw Brandy. He had stepped out of his

villa, a glass in his hand, but his smile hardened as he saw Tory. He came forward, drawing her out of the disembarking stream. His silvery eyes touched the bronze maillot, traveled to Zan.

"Here's the salve," Zan told her. He had bandaged her cut on the way back with a detachment that puzzled Tory. "When you can, expose the cut to sun and air."

"Have we gained a doctor?" Brandy drawled. "Or is this one of the beach boys?"

Nothing for it but to introduce them, explaining that Zan was a new member of the tour. He excused himself, exchanging mutually cool remarks with Brandy, saying he had to make final arrangements for his business while he was away, and turned to unload the big box of snorkeling gear from the baggage compartment.

Brandy sipped his old-fashioned and surveyed the mostly bared bodies of the tour members as they wandered off to their quarters. "I trust these swims aren't going to be a regular part of the schedule," he observed. "I much prefer my fellow man in his garments."

"Which I need to change into." Tory started off. He caught her hand.

"Hello, love," he said, features relaxing. He turned up her face and kissed her. "I carried through some extremely valuable business, but I've missed you sadly!" He stroked her cheek, let his hand rest a moment on the pulse of her throat. His eyes smoldered like blue flame under ice. "I wish this were our honeymoon, darling. I want everyone to know you belong to me."

Especially Zan? There was a harshness in Brandy's expression that made Tory decide this wasn't the time to protest that verb, "belong."

~❦ VI ❦~

As they journeyed to Uxmal the next day, Theron kept stopping the bus at points where he suspected there might be good birding opportunities. An abandoned lime quarry yielded dozens of turquoise-browed motmots. These relatives of the quetzal perched above their deep holes in the sides of the quarry and swung their long tails like pendulums. A black hawk flew over and the Summervilles spotted a male Amazon kingfisher.

The next stop by a river turned up a tree full of parrots. Tory was satiated by then and feeling the heat, as were several other people. At the fifth halt only Theron, the Callahans, Morgan, and Zan bundled off to trudge along a marsh.

Brandy, who hadn't gotten off at all, glanced after the trekkers and shook his head. "Mad dogs and birders," he paraphrased. "Your beachcomber friend at least seems to be earnest. I'll confess that I laid his interest in the tour to being enamored of you, but perhaps I wronged him."

Strange, but being around Brandy for long periods, trying to live up to his expectations, was

61

becoming a strain, a burden, not a challenge as pleasing him had once been. When their romance began, she'd been so proud of his approval that she'd felt she must try hard to be the woman he believed her. The close proximity of the trip, however, was beginning to make her nervous. She had never been one to much question or restrain her impulses. Having to constantly think ahead to the consequences and his reaction made her feel pressed down by an increasingly heavy weight so that she acted under the sort of resistance she felt when coming out of the sea after that long delightfully buoyant swim with Zan.

"What's the matter, Victoria?" Brandy, with the back of his thumb, smoothed away her frown. "You seem a bit forlorn."

"Just tired. I didn't sleep too well."

"Try to get a nap after lunch, my sweet. Can't have you down-spirited." Brandy squeezed her hand and returned to his portfolio.

Tory gazed unseeingly at her bird guide. *Be happy*. That was always Brandy's message to her. It was as if she was supposed to be an unfailing source of perpetual euphoria, create a lightheartedness he could enjoy when it suited him.

She couldn't. And, she decided, tightening her jaw, she wasn't going to try! Brandy was going to have to know her as she was, in every mood, and if he couldn't accept her, it was much better they both learn that now.

Hacienda Uxmal, though, would have delighted the most sated traveler. Entering a smallish door shaded by vines and trees, Tory gazed at vistas of polished tile and mellow adobe arches surrounding a courtyard filled with giant trees and blooming with wisteria, bougainvillea, and a rainbow of other flowers, shrubs, and vines. The reception hall displayed magnificent hangings, carvings, and pictures as well as immense bright pottery animals and angels. The staircase was ornamented with gleaming tile and guarded by a handsome black wrought-iron balustrade that continued in a railing going around the arch-windowed balcony on the second floor.

Tory and Elspeth's room proved to be up that stair and along the terrace overlooking the pool. Elspeth wanted a shower and rest before lunch, but Tory was so beguiled by the once private great house that had been renovated into this graciously elegant hostelry that she did only basic unpacking in their spacious shady room before going out to explore.

The huge building enclosing the courtyard was creamy golden adobe, its simplicity enhanced by brilliant tile, intricately carved wooden shutters, graceful repetition of arches, and wrought-iron filigree. As Tory wandered from one terrace to another, she found countless alcoves and recesses where flowers and plants, pottery or carvings, were an endless feast to the eye. Groupings of heavy wood or cane chairs and tables were scattered about and the vast spreading trees grew so close that Tory would have loved to scramble out on the branches.

As she passed the dining room, tantalizing odors reminded her that it had been hours since breakfast and she was hungry. She hurried back to her room, showered, and changed into a white blouse and full skirt. Elspeth, yawning, listened to Tory's enraptured account and dressed, too.

"That ceiling fan's better than a lullaby," she said as the big blades revolved slowly. "I could get addicted to this place."

"Better enjoy it. I hear Palenque's what can be euphemistically labeled rustic."

The tour people were sitting in the raised section of the dining room. Tory smothered a gasp as she saw Zan and Brandy deep in conversation. They rose to greet the women, who were immediately seated by two white-clad waiters.

"The chicken pibil's supposed to be delicious," said Brandy. "Or you might like eggs Motul." The menu had venison, turkey, ham, and a tempting choice of desserts.

The others ordered chicken pibil, but Tory had the eggs, which proved to be lightly poached, resting on a crisped tortilla and covered with peas, spicy red sauce, and cubed ham. Brandy insisted she try his chicken. Zan said it was doused with *achiote*, a fruit native to Yucatán and Chiapas, and bitter orange, then wrapped in green leaves and roasted slowly to mouth-watering succulence. Pork and armadillo cooked in the same way were also called pibil.

There was an excellent salad and squashlike *chayote* besides the first course of delicate chicken soup. Through all this and the caramel custard they had for dessert, Brandy and Zan talked about CEDAM and its salvaging operations.

Besides locating and exploring a number of wrecked ships, including *La Nicolasa*, which went down in 1527, a ship of Montejo, who founded Mérida, CEDAM had explored underwater archaeological sites. Chichén Itzá's *cenote* was the most famous of these.

"We brought up thousands of things," remembered Zan, shaking his head in wonder. "Wooden furniture a thousand years old in flawless condition, pots, jade, incense, painted gourds, several stone idols, and five absolutely marvelous carved stone jaguars. But it's tough in those *cenotes*. Water's cloudy and loaded with bacteria."

"I've heard there's still a lot left in the Chichén Itzá *cenote*," said Brandy.

Zan nodded. "Pablo Bush, the founder of CEDAM, thinks most of the treasure's still down there."

"Fascinating," mused Brandy, giving Zan a warm slow smile. "I envy your share in recovering such antiquities."

"I've loved it," said Zan with a quick glance at Tory. "Going on an expedition means leaving my business for weeks, of course, and working at my own expense, but it's a way of thanking this country for being good to me." He cocked an eyebrow at Tory. "That may sound improvident, but since I'm not married there's no one to goad me along the straight-and-narrow business-first trail."

"It's an estimable thing, recovering national treasures," said Tory in a stiff tone. "But when a person has the only service shop along a beach, I do feel he has an obligation to see it's staffed. With someone bilingual enough to rent snorkels."

"Gregorio can rent snorkels."

"Only, presumably, to Yucatán males."

"Maybe I should get a *yanqui* wife," said Zan. "She wouldn't be scared of *gringas* and she could straighten out my bookkeeping."

"What bookkeeping?" scorned Tory.

Zan sighed. "So it's that obvious?" he asked sadly.

Tory snorted. Brandy gave her a mildly reproving glance. "How can a U.S. citizen own a business in Mexico?"

"I have a Yucatán partner who owns fifty-one percent of the enterprise."

"How does he feel about *gringas*?" Tory demanded.

"Loves 'em." Zan grinned.

"Then maybe he should be tending the shop."

"Luis Herrera de Castillo has ranches, plantations, and an interest in half-a-dozen resorts." Zan shrugged. "My outfit's about his smallest potato, I'd reckon, but he's a diver and member of CEDAM."

"Why, I know Don Luis," said Brandy. "I've supplied a number of rare items for his collections. A gentleman of rare discrimination."

"He can afford it." Zan's tone was dry. "Are you

going to the sound-and-light show at the ruins tonight?"

"Sounds a bore," Brandy said, grimacing. "Victoria, you won't mind if I do some long-distance phoning and a few letters before we plunge into the wilds? Theron tells me there's no telephone at our Palenque headquarters and that the mail pickup is, to understate it, dubious."

"You certainly mustn't go if you won't enjoy it," Tory said, but added a bit defiantly, "It may be 'tourist,' but that's what I am."

Brandy also opted out of the late-afternoon bird-walk that skirted the principal ruins and followed a grown-over road that led past the crumbling Witch's House above the scattered pillars of the understandably named Phallic Temple.

Theron recounted the legend that the witch had hatched a dwarf from an egg, and together, in one night, they built the great pyramid that towered over the magnificent complex. This dwarf later became the ruler of Uxmal.

"The miracle is how anyone believed that story, ever," said Zan. "There are openings all along the face of the pyramid of the magician leading to the earlier temples around which the fifth and last is raised. These constructions took place during a period of at least three hundred years."

Tory made a face at him. "Much more fun to have a witch-child make it."

"You prefer the dream of the enchanter to the reality?"

"Yes, and why not?"

Those disturbingly changeable green-gray eyes probed hers. She felt as if he'd touched her with his long brown hands, fought an inner trembling that threatened to become outwardly apparent.

"I thought you a practical lady who rated business over enchantment."

"Just because I think having a business incurs certain basic responsibilities, you've no right to cast me as an insensitive clod." She stalked off to peer through the scope Theron had focused on what he called a blue-black grassquit.

"Variable seedeater," muttered Elspeth, but softly enough that only Tory heard.

Theron, up ahead, announced that it was time to start back. "But if anyone's really keen on ruins," he said, "there's a small interesting one half-overgrown with jungle not far off the second well-marked trail. You might want to go there after the tour of the main ruins tomorrow."

That sounded good to Tory. She preferred being able to look at something without a crowd pressing in, feeling and experiencing the mood and atmosphere, scents and shadings. There was no time when a guide was describing periods and facts, and hordes of tourists were dashing about or listening to *their* guides, to just quietly wait on the spirits, listen, and dream. And she loved to dream, whatever Alexander the Great thought!

After an excellent dinner of venison at a table she and Brandy shared with the Callahans and Summervilles, Tory started with Elspeth and about half the tour members for the sound-and-light show at the ruins. Zan had disappeared and Tory wondered with a twinge of something very like jealousy if he'd gone somewhere with Morgan. He'd been at her table that evening and they'd seemed to be having a much livelier discussion than the one Brandy and Mark Summerville were having on tax havens.

A nondescript brown and buff dog rose from a watchful position at the side of the road and approached Tory with a wistfully flourishing corkscrew tail. He plainly hoped for a caress while fearing a kick. He was not at all like the small tan handsome short-haired dogs she had seen in Yucatán.

"Buenas noches," she told him. *"¿Cómo estas, perrito?"*

He hopefully waved his ragged tail. Even in the dusk, cinnamon eye tufts gave him a perpetually questioning look. He fell in with the group, sticking close to Tory, and trotted along to the ruins.

It was dark by the time they reached the thicket kiosk. No camera tripods were allowed, but Mark Summerville had his unipod, which looked like a rather ugly chromium walking stick. A guide with a flashlight escorted them up steel steps that ran up the side of the ruins like a fire escape. Eluding the guide, the mongrel ran nimbly up the metallically resounding stairs and avoided notice till the group was seated and the guide was gone. Stealthily then, the dog crept up to lie in front of Tory as red and green lights played on the masks of the rain god Chac that flanked the 150 steep steps leading to the temple on the top.

For almost an hour, voices and music told the story of Uxmal, the thrice-built, while lights played on latticed stone fretwork, entwined serpents, the jagged faces of Chac on the pyramid, Nunnery Quadrangle, Temple of Venus, and the Palace of the Governor. The need for rain recurred over and over, the prayers of the people to Chac, for there were no *cenotes* near Uxmal, no rivers or lakes. Natural hollows were coated with lime to catch the scanty rainfall, but always and ever Chac must be wooed and worshiped for his anger meant drought and death.

At the end, when the music built to a crescendo, the dog, who had been napping peacefully through the show and Mark Summerville's photo-taking, lifted his head and howled dolefully.

"I wonder if he comes all the time." Elspeth chuckled.

The dog followed them back to Hacienda Uxmal, but stopped outside the hall as if he knew his place. "Good night, dog," Tory told him with a pat as he settled down, his scruffy countenance between his paws.

"He's probably got fleas," warned Brandy from the arch. "Come have a drink, love, and dance with me awhile. I need to relax after all those phone calls. Wrestling with long distance out of here has to be experienced to be believed."

That sort of thing could be terribly frustrating, but Tory, whose feet hurt quite apart from the deep coral scratch, couldn't help but think that if Brandy had gone birding that afternoon or trekked over to the sound-and-light show, he wouldn't now feel like dancing. He slipped her arm under his and bore her off to a table under the palms and trailing wisteria.

Between sips of a frozen lime daiquiri, she described the show. Though Brandy's eyes were intent on her, he was plainly not interested in Uxmal's history. The moment she finished her drink, he took her hands and drew her up.

"The dance floor's postage stamp and the music's frenetic," he said in her ear, brushing her cheek with his lips in that slow lingering practiced way that made her breath come unevenly while her blood felt heavy with warm honey. "But I want to hold you in my arms, darling."

Her cut foot throbbed and she started to plead weariness, but then, through the arches leading into the cantina, she saw Zan whirling Morgan, laughing down at her uptilted, dramatically appealing face. She had to be ten years older, but that clearly wasn't bothering either of them.

Pain curved through Tory like a subtly twisting blade, though she quickly told herself that whom Zan danced with was no concern of hers. She let Brandy swing her into the dance, forced herself to laugh and chatter. Soon the old magnetism flowed between them as Brandy held her in a cherishingly firm grasp. He was easily the most striking man on the floor, as handsome in his way as Zan, a massive eagle compared to Zan's slighter wilder kestrel or falcon.

His silver eyes glowed as he led with a force that made her tremulously aware of his tall, splendidly proportioned body. "I overestimated my waiting powers," he whispered. "I thought this trip would give us a chance to know each other at close range, but it's also driving me wild!"

"Brandy . . ." She tried to draw away, but he went on insistently. "Sweetheart, let's rent a car and drive back to Mérida, get married, and have our honeymoon at Cancún or Cozumel." He drew her into an alcove. "Why wait? Please, darling!"

Panic flared in Tory, strangely a part of the tempestuous feelings coursing through her. She turned her mouth away from his. He brought her face upward, laughing huskily.

"I was crazy to think I could spend three weeks with you, Victoria, before we were married. I'll get a ring in Mérida, we can even take your aunt back for the ceremony if you insist. But let's do it! Let's do it, love."

His mouth sought hers, though Tory resisted, caught in a smothering drowning weakness. But as the kiss began, a voice beside them said, "Forgive me for barging in, but I especially crave this dance with this lady."

~✺ VII ✺~

Zan offered Brandy Morgan's hand. His green eyes seemed almost black in the shadows. "I brought you a partner," he said, as Morgan bestowed a dazzling smile on Brandy.

Without being rude to her, there was little Brandy could do but release Tory, still breathless from his kiss, shaken at his sudden insistent proposal. The musicians were playing "La Peregrina," the liltingly sensuous song Zan's mariachi friends had played at Akumal.

"You asked for this tune," she accused, keeping as far from him as she could and still stay in rhythm.

He smiled and for a moment let his face rest against her hair. "I ask for what I want, Tory."

"I'm sure you do."

Slowly, compellingly, he drew her closer. "You might be surprised at how often I get it."

"I wouldn't. Anyone with your—"

"Frankness?" His eyes danced, and he swept her into a dipping swirl. "Candor? Simplicity?"

"Nerve!"

He shrugged resignedly, sun-bleached brows lifting. "Is that what you'd call it? All right. Finish your sentence."

"I've forgotten it. You're impossible!"

"Presumably your fiancé *is* possible—yet you certainly didn't seem to be enjoying your sojourn in the alcove."

"So you chivalrously came to the rescue."

"No. I wanted you in my arms."

He spoke quietly, but something in his tone sent a shock through her like a lightning flash. Battling it, she said in a tone that was supposed to be light but came out bitter, "You seemed delighted with the lady you had."

"Morgan? She's great company. Mercifully past all the girlish nonsense."

"Yes. Being forty should help with that." It slipped out. Tory could have bitten her tongue at the catty remark even before Zan's face closed.

"I think people usually become more what they are by nature. Morgan, I suspect, has always been generous and zestful."

"I'm sure she has," said Tory stiffly.

They danced wordlessly to the end of the number. Zan returned her to Brandy who suggested they all have a drink together. Tory didn't feel able just then to gracefully endure Morgan's sparkle. Even more strongly, she didn't want to give Brandy another chance to urge abandoning the tour and getting married at once.

"I'm really tired," she said, refusing the chair

Brandy held for her. "If you'll excuse me, I'll go on up."

"I'll take you to your room," Brandy said, frowning slightly.

Tory shook her head. "Don't bother, it's right up the stairs. Good night, everybody. See you in the morning." She smiled and hurried for the stairway.

The ceiling fan revolved in a gentle drowsy hum as Tory opened the door. Elspeth was already asleep. Quietly, Tory had a shower and slid under the crisp sheets, her weary body luxuriating in the comfort. She was glad to have avoided an argument with Brandy, for she had absolutely no intention of quitting the tour. She would have gladly married Brandy before the trip, but his attitudes and behavior had begun to worry her. She wasn't a bird fanatic, but she wasn't about to miss the glories of Palenque down in the rain forests. This trip might well be her last as a single person and she meant to enjoy it.

The phone rang. She clambered across the bed for it, caught it before a second ring could disturb Elspeth, and spoke under her breath.

"Yes?"

"Darling, won't you come out on the terrace a minute?"

Brandy. Surprised at the depths of her annoyance, Tory swallowed to get it under control. "I'm already in bed and I'm awfully tired."

"Too tired to discuss our marriage?"

"I don't see why we should discuss it at all right now, Brandy."

Silence. Then, with an edge to his voice, "Does that mean you won't consider dropping this stupid tour and going to Mérida?"

"You didn't have to come," Tory reminded him. "It clearly isn't the kind of thing you like, so perhaps you should forget it. But it's my present to Elspeth. I do want her at my wedding. And I wouldn't dream of asking her to skip part of the trip."

After a long pause Brandy said in silkily furious tones, "Marriage—at least to me—doesn't seem exactly high priority for you, Victoria."

"I just can't see any reason to suddenly change all our plans."

"What I want doesn't matter?"

Urbane, sophisticated Brandy sounding like a spoiled child? Baffled at how to respond, Tory didn't try now to keep anger from her voice.

"It seems to me that you're bored with the tour and see getting married and having our honeymoon as a way to use up the block of time you've set aside. I can sympathize with your deciding this isn't your thing, but you've no right deciding that for me."

She could almost see him staring at the phone in shocked disbelief. "Could the handsome Alexander have anything to do with your devotion to the tour?"

"At least he's not bored with everything." Tory took a deep breath. "I don't want to talk about it now, Brandy. Elspeth's asleep, and as I said before leaving, I really am tired."

No reply for a tense moment. "Go to sleep then," Brandy said in a ruefully tender way. "See you at breakfast, love."

He wouldn't be on the six-o'clock birdwalk. Tory cradled the phone. She expected to lie awake chewing over her resentments at Brandy and Zan but the purring fan lulled her into sighing and snuggling deeper into the smooth cool pillows. She thought of Zan's arms guiding her in the dance and then she was asleep.

At the shrill of the alarm, Tory and Elspeth were up and dressed, assembled with most of the party outside the hotel as dawn began to finger the sky. Zan and Morgan were joking, in contrast to the groggy though good-humored silence of the rest. Neither of them looked sleepy, but Tory wondered how late they'd been up. Theron appeared, lugging the scope, and Zan took it for him.

As they trudged down the road toward the ruins, the black and buff mongrel rose from beneath a bush and approached humbly, waving his preposterous tail.

"Sorry, boy," said Theron. "Dogs and birdwatching don't mix." He tried to shoo the animal away, but it seemed to know Theron wouldn't really hurt him and dodged in and out of the birders with great agility till he reached Tory. He pressed against her knees and gazed up at her in confidence.

"Stay here," she told him, pointing to the road-side. He licked her adjuring finger.

"Git, you monster," snapped Elspeth, stamping her foot at him.

He moved out of range, but slunk close to Tory. "Go ahead," she told Theron. "Maybe I can get him to stay here." The group moved on. Tory led the dog back to the arch of the hotel and coaxed him to lie down. "Stay!" she commanded.

Swishing his tail in the dust, he watched her with guileless adoration. His bones stuck out and Tory resolved to get him a treat after the kitchen opened.

"*Adiós, perrito.*" She gave him a pat and started off, but he was on his feet at once.

Halting, she stared at him in a quandary. She couldn't bring herself to hit or swear at him. A soft chuckle sounded behind her.

"You go, *señorita.*" Narciso's white smile flashed. He was amused at her problem. "I make *el perro* stay."

"Oh, *gracias*, Narciso. *Muchas gracias.*" With a heartfelt smile of gratitude, she gave the dog a parting caress and hurried to catch up with the group.

She found them halfway to the ruins, binoculars at the ready, trying to glimpse a blue bunting but settling for a black-throated bobwhite. It took half an hour, stopping to admire ruddy ground doves, a dusky-capped flycatcher, and American redstart, to reach the old road to the left of the main ruins.

They were starting across the clearing when, from the corner of her eye, Tory glimpsed black-and-buff. Not in a tree, either. "Here's your friend," called Zan.

Tory glared at the dog, who let his tail move back and forth in tentative greeting. The Bowdries and Cunninghams detoured around him as if fearing mange. Theron groaned.

"What are we going to do about you, mutt?"

Since Tory had let him follow the night before, she felt responsible for the dilemma. Besides, she went birding for the walk rather than primarily for sighting species. "I'll keep him with me," she volunteered. "I can ramble toward the Witch's House and go back to the hotel when I'm ready."

"You're sure?" Theron asked.

Tory nodded and took the side trail. Black-and-buff almost turned cartwheels in his haste to escort her. She gave him a scratch between his pricked-up ears. "Narciso must have thought you'd forgotten me and turned you loose. But that's all right. It's a nice morning and I never spot half the birds everyone else does anyway." His speeded tail wag agreed that she was indeed perspicacious to choose his company over a birdwalk.

"Let's go find that second well-marked trail that Theron said led to some nice little ruins. Then we'll go back to the hotel and see if I can't get you something nice to eat."

Perrito lolled his tongue and enthusiastically agreed with anything she might then or ever propose. They walked through the pleasant cool, past the tumbled phalluses and the more distant ruined walls of the Witch's House, moved into dense growth chopped back from a narrow road.

Tory was on the watch for some kind of sign with an arrow pointing A LAS RUINAS, and though she passed several side paths, none were what she'd remotely classify as well-marked. The road deteriorated into a track dimly visible through undergrowth. Determined now to find the ruins, Tory pushed through giant weeds and vines, emerged abruptly on a road that was obviously much-used though it was dirt.

"Maybe there's not a sign," Tory suggested to the panting dog. The sun was up now and the refreshing air of dawn was heating rapidly. "Maybe it's just one of those paths we saw way back there."

She glanced at her watch. Not quite seven. If she picked the right trail and hurried, she should be back for eight-o'clock breakfast. Often, for Tory, objectives that weren't too important at the start became so as she encountered problems. Mildly interested in the ruins before, she was now determined to find them.

Once back near the Witch's House, Tory again started up the road. One distinct trail. The next one surely couldn't be termed well-marked . . . but this third path was clear enough.

"*Aqui*," she called to the dog, who plunged past her, nimbly avoiding spiky stubs that thrust up from the ground.

The trees, though not extremely tall, grew thick and close, here and there twisting roots about ancient traces of wall. Perrito sniffed around one large shallow hole partly lined with rock, and Tory thought it must have been one of the water-catching *aguadas*.

It was cool out of the sun and she was seeing more birds than she ever had on an organized walk. To her surprised pleasure, she recognized the notched brownish tail and yellow belly of a tropical kingbird, and a few minutes later could remember how it differed from a social flycatcher perched to her right with his white-striped head.

When the tour began, she'd never expected to distinguish between the various flycatchers, but she was learning; and though she could enjoy birds without knowing their names, it *was* rather fun to know that the Altamira oriole she'd just glimpsed was considerably larger than the similar hooded oriole and had only one white wing bar to the hooded's two.

On the slope ahead a wall rose above the remains of an arched passage through which Tory could see daylight. Stones were scattered amid carvings and pediments, the gray-white limestone entwined by vines and manacling roots. The structure must have been of some size and elegance, but only the forest knew it now.

Tory approached it cautiously, testing each foot-hold. Loose rock and debris slid about her laced-above-the-ankle walking shoes, but she tried not to grab at trees or bushes for support. Theron had warned them that there were several toxic plants in the region and she had no wish for a grossly swollen arm. Perrito scrambled ahead of her, snuffing under logs and accumulations of rubble.

The small arched gallery was just ahead. The tops of Mayan arches were not oval but like flat-topped pyramids. Festooned with vines, this one small part was all that remained roofed and usable out of what once had covered the whole slope. The approach was very steep here. Tory planted one foot on a large stone and swung the other toward a cluster of thick roots.

One of the roots moved. An ugly pitted head struck at Tory's foot where it was suspended in midair. Paralyzed, she watched as the snake uncoiled from the roots.

With a thunderous barking, Perrito dropped on the snake from above. The reptile's head lashed back. The dog yelped but held on, shaking his enemy back and forth till it stopped moving. Perrito let it drop and trotted to Tory, licking her hands anxiously.

"Are you hurt, boy?" she asked, shaking with terrified reaction, absolutely dewed with chill sweat. She looked Perrito over, but his hair and dark hide obscured any marks. "You're a warrior," she praised him. "But let's get back to the hotel and get some serum for you if you need it. I hate to look at that thing, but I suppose I'll have to describe it to find out if it's poisonous."

Stepping forward, she gazed at the mangled creature, fought a wave of nausea. It was yellow beneath the mouth and seemed to have two pair of nostrils.

"*Curatro narices,*" she remembered. "Perrito, that's a fer-de-lance. They're dangerous! Come on!"

"What's the matter, love?"

She whirled to see Brandy step through the arch.

~✦ VIII ✦~

As they hurried along the trail, Brandy clearly thinking it was a lot of fuss over a mongrel, he said that he'd gotten restless and decided to have a walk before breakfast. "I was quite pleased with myself for discovering that hidden little ruin," he said as Tory almost ran beside Perrito. "How did you come across it? And where's the rest of the expedition?"

Tory was explaining when Zan plunged into view. "I heard the dog," he called, changing from a lope to a stride. "Sounded like trouble."

"It was," Tory shouted. "Perrito killed a fer-de-lance. I think it bit him."

Zan whistled up the dog and looked him over, straightened with a shake of the head. "A dog his size probably wouldn't die, but the venom could make him mighty sick. Chances are that precious little snake juice penetrated the hair and hide." His eyes seemed almost black as he stared at her. "Praise be the dog found the snake instead of you."

"I was fixing to step on it when Perrito jumped right on top of that horrid thing." Tory shuddered.

She smoothed her champion's scruffy hair. "Could we get some serum or something?"

"I think he'd rather have a turkey drumstick," said Zan. "If he needs serum, Tory, he'd never last till we get it. Let's just take good care of him and hope for the best. I'll carry him to the hotel and we'll find someone to feed him and keep him quiet."

Brandy made a disgusted sound as Zan picked up the ungainly animal. "Good Lord, Ericson! What a fuss over as unprepossessing a bone bag as I've seen in all my life!"

"Quite a spunky bone bag," Zan said. "If Tory had been bitten way back here, she could have passed out before she reached help.

So the canine waif was borne gently back to the grand hotel. Brandy fidgeted in annoyance and hunger, but Tory stayed with Perrito till Zan returned with a boy of nine or ten. "Álvaro's the head gardener's son and he'll be glad to tend our dog. His mother knows some herbs that help with snakebite and she's already brewing them up."

"Thank you," Tory said, vastly relieved.

Perrito still seemed fine, but she shrank from the thought of his dying for her. She shook hands with Álvaro, who made earnest promises both verbally and with soft brown eyes. Zan lifted the dog and started down the paved walk leading through giant trees to a number of typical whitewashed oval Mayan huts with their neat thatches.

"That's done, then!" Brandy's tone was over-hearty. "Let's wash and get to breakfast, Victoria. I'm famished."

"Go ahead," Tory advised. "I want to see Perrito settled."

"Darling, for heaven's sake!"

Tory kept walking. She met Señora Ortiz, who indeed had a pot steaming, and saw the dog comfortably stretched out under the shade of the ramada.

"Please tell her I'll pay," Tory whispered.

"I've taken care of that."

"But he saved me!"

Zan's jaw flexed for a moment. Telling the Ortizes good-bye, he steered Tory outside. "I'm a collector, too," he said as they walked to the hotel. "I like creatures of valor. That scroungy mutt *is* valiant and I'm coming back here to get him after the tour ends."

"You will?" cried Tory, catching his hands in delight. "I'm so glad! I've been wishing since last night there were some way I could be sure he had a home."

"He will," Zan promised. He grinned and gathered Tory's hands against his chest. "You can fly down and bring him a bone anytime you like."

"Victoria," called Brandy from the hotel entrance. "You'd better hurry. They stop serving in ten minutes."

Zan made a face. "Bet he even organizes his lovemaking."

Tory ignored that. Zan had been wonderful about Perrito, but he was a trial in other ways.

She sped past Brandy, freshened up, and made it into the restaurant just in time to order.

The Pyramid of the Magician towering up from rounded sides toward thunderclouds that were the manifestation of Chac; red painted hands on the ceiling of one building in the Nunnery Quadrangle, heavenly hands of the god Zamna whose name translates to "Dew of Heaven."

They had hired an official guide who proudly told them that the four buildings in the quad were considered the greatest example of Mayan skill in creating a complex of buildings, while the Palace of the Governor, to which they next journeyed, was called the most outstanding single Mayan building.

This palace had a plain lower facade topped by a ten-foot-high frieze worked with Chac masks, crosses, elegantly headdressed figures, thatched huts, wreaths, thrones, and other motifs.

"Pure Puuc style," murmured Beata, blue eyes glowing. "Puuc means hill and is a term for the architecture of this single hilly part of Yucatán and its cities of Uxmal, Sayil, and Kabah."

"In the frieze alone," proclaimed the guide, "there are twenty thousand dressed stones weighing from fifty-five to one hundred and seventy-five pounds. Those are the remains of the ball court between the palace and the Nunnery; when we go up on the platform, you'll see the remains of the Dwarf's House, a pyramid that was as large as if not larger than the Pyramid of the Magician."

The stairs of the palace were easy, and Tory got pictures of the Temple of the Turtles and the Dovecotes, so named because the remaining pyramidal shapes of the roof comb resembled dovecotes.

"I like these buildings better than those at Chichén Itzá," said Frieda Callahan. "They're much more graceful."

Tory nodded. "You're much more aware of human sacrifice at Chichén—the *cenote,* that frieze with the beheaded man in the ball court, the huge enclosure for bodies of sacrificial victims that was completely carved with skulls."

Brandy was down in front of the palace admiring a sleek double-jaguar sculpture. "I've seen similar small ones in jade," he told Tory. "Worth a fortune. This had the classic simplicity found in China and Egypt that looks modern because it's so streamlined."

"Seri ironwood and Eskimo carvings have the same clean lines," said Elspeth.

"But they're still being made," Brandy pointed out. "When arts are lost or abandoned, remaining specimens will multiply in value, but except for the rarest Aleut and Tlingit work, it's not worth my time." He slipped Tory's arm through his and drew her along. "Why the furrowed brow, my sweet?"

"It's too bad that art has to be *dead* before it's worth much."

He shrugged. "I'd rather call it survival of the

finest, the search for what's rare. There's no pride in owning what everyone can have."

"But surely there are better reasons than exclusivity for admiring or treasuring something."

Brandy heaved a good-natured sigh. "You'll agree that I'm fond of Everest?"

Remembering the very shaggy dirty white beast, Tory nodded, suppressing her opinion that he looked like a cross between a dust mop and a yak.

"As I may have told you, he's a Lhasa Apso from the Himalayas. There are only a few in the whole United States. I couldn't possibly derive the same satisfaction from owning an ordinary dog even if it was in every other way as desirable a pet as Everest."

"Then it seems to me that what's important isn't the dog but his rarity."

Brandy nodded.

"I think that's sad." Tory hated the tremor in her voice. "Really sad."

"Why?" Brandy's slim brows raised, and he took her hand, drawing her after the rest of the group, who were starting back through the almost obliterated ball court.

"Because that's putting more importance on a quality, a purely accidental one, than on what something is as a whole and of itself." Tory bit her lip, then tossed back her head challengingly. "If you feel like that, Brandy, I don't see how I can be the right wife for you. I'm not especially intelligent or talented or beautiful—"

They were concealed from the party by shrubby

growth. Brandy drew her into his arms, found her lips, and kissed her in that wooing melting way that always swept away her doubts. "You're wrong, Victoria," he murmured, kissing her ear and cheek and forehead in teasing admonishing playfulness. "You make me feel. You touch my heart. No other woman has ever done that." He laughed softly. "Enchantment, that's what it is."

"That's so—so fragile."

"I'm not going to change," he reassured her. "So long as you don't!" He kissed her till the nagging little worries faded in the comforting strength of his arms.

But as they walked on, Tory felt a wave of anxiety. What had once made her proud and happy, given her confidence in herself as a woman, was the fact that Brandy, with his vast experience and desirability, had chosen her. Now she felt under a sort of threat; if she ceased to fulfill his expectations, there was nothing solid to hold them together.

It all seemed to depend on the novelty of her unconscious effect on him. That sounded romantically magical, but it was treacherous magic; just as it turned Cinderella into a princess, it could send her back to sob among the ashes. Tory wondered how she could breathe freely, move with any ease, if she was constantly fearful of breaking a spell.

They assembled next morning in the predawn dimness, yawning amid their luggage. Tory had

visited Perrito the evening before, bringing chicken she'd saved from her dinner. His foot was swollen, but Señora Ortiz was dosing him with herbs and was sure he'd recover. When Tory tried to leave money for the dog's care, the plump dark-eyed woman shook her head, explaining in broken English that Zan had paid.

Tory had thanked him that morning, but he'd only given her a sleepy good-natured grin and turned to answer some question of Morgan's. They had been in the cantina last night. So had Tory and Brandy, but after a few dances and one margarita, Tory pleaded weariness and went to her room.

The only good thing about Morgan's association with Zan was that theoretically it should have given Elspeth a chance to talk more with Theron. She wasn't doing this, though, was actually stationing herself at the end of the column on birdwalks, asking no questions and asserting no identifications.

"I see Theron shooting you baffled glances," Tory had said to her aunt as they dressed that morning and hurried to get their luggage out in the hall for the porter. "Why don't you ask him something now and then?"

"I can't," said Elspeth, woefully shaking her head. "If I say anything, I'll get carried away and be contentious. I've already done too much of that."

At last all the luggage was stowed away and Narciso stashed the boxed breakfasts aboard. In

order to reach Palenque by dark, they had to leave two hours before the hotel served breakfast.

Brandy appeared as Narciso opened the door of Dina for boarding. "Had to make a few last-minute calls," he said. He spoke softly in Tory's ear. "It's not too late to go to Mérida, my love."

She had no answer for that and didn't try to find one.

As near darkness softened to gray and flushed with dawn, Theron passed out white cardboard boxes containing two cheese and meat sandwiches, two hard-boiled eggs, crisply sweet *pan dulce*, an orange, and a banana. Hacienda Uxmal was making sure its early-departing guests wouldn't go hungry. Tory worked through the sandwiches but saved the rest.

It was a steady drive to Champotón, where they had fresh good seafood in the restaurant part of the bus station, a long open-sided thatched roof over corrugated metal building. Departures and arrivals were written on blackboards by a ticket booth, but no one seemed to be either coming or going. The green waters of the Gulf of Mexico lapped on the beach near the station and only the knowledge that it was still a long way to Palenque made anyone ready to leave.

"I've been working on an animals' sound song in the little Spanish I know," plump golden Mildred Halliday said to Tory as they were having the dessert of fresh fruit and melon. "Your aunt says you're good at fitting words to familiar tunes. Could you help me? There's a party tomorrow

night and it'd be fun to have this ready. If I just had my guitar!"

"Maybe we can borrow one at Palenque," Tory said hopefully. "I used to compose doggerel for our high-school skits, but I doubt if I can be much help, especially in Spanish. I'll be glad to try, though."

Brandy cast her an annoyed look, but she ignored him. Hadn't he worked at his portfolio all morning? She didn't want to chatter incessantly, but it was damping to feel she shouldn't break into his concentration to point out the small handsome horses they were beginning to see, or sandpipers, plover, several kinds of egret, heron, osprey, and chachalaca.

"I'll be back when Mildred and I complete her masterpiece," Tory told Brandy as they got on the bus.

"I worked all morning to clear the afternoon for conversation," he said.

"Now isn't that lovely," caroled Morgan. "May I sit by you, Mr. Sherrod? I've got so much curiosity about your business. It sounds absolutely fascinating."

Mildred and Tory moved to the back of the bus where Mildred produced a shorthand tablet with several pages of smudged and crossed-out writing.

> *¿Qué canta la paloma*
> *En su nido en la loma?*
> *Cu-cu-cu-curuuuu!*
> *¿Qué canta el zopilote*
> *Cerca del mogote?*
> *Scree-scree-scree!*

¿Qué canta el tecolote?
¿Qué grita el coyote?
Who-who-who-who-who-whoooo!

"This is cute!" Tory laughed, humming, trying to fit syllables to a singable rhythm. "I think it'd go real well to a modified 'El Rancho Grande.'"

"Let's see . . ." Mildred hummed, then sang in a sweet low-pitched voice, looked inquiringly at Tory.

"Sounds good." Tory nodded.

This *was* nice! If Mildred could sing and play during the week they'd spend in Palenque, where there'd be few entertainments once night hid the birds, it would give her a place.

They ran out of birds and began inventing verses with burros, horses, cats, and dogs. While they were working on the *perro's* "Bow-wow-wow-wow-wow," Mildred nibbled on her pencil.

"I've read somewhere that the dogs of the ancient Mayas *couldn't* bark. I wonder if any of that breed are still around."

"We can ask Narciso," Tory suggested. She noticed that Mildred was bedewed with perspiration and that she was getting uncomfortably warm herself. Holding a hand to the air-conditioning vent confirmed her fear. "Good grief! Dina's lost her cool."

Theron rose to confirm this. "Narciso can probably fix it tonight, but it'll take hours and there's no place you folks could get in out of the heat if we stopped now. We'll just have to open windows and think about the birds we're going to see in Palenque. There'll be the three kinds of Mexican toucans, the big keel-billed, the smaller emerald toucanet, and the collared aricari. You may sight a dozen kinds of flycatchers and there are almost that many sorts of hummingbirds. There'll be more parrots and trogons and motmots and lots of tanagers."

"Will you guarantee a bright-rumped attila?" called Mark Summerville.

"We have enough time for you to see just about any bird you really want to." Theron grinned. "I was here last summer and saw a hundred and twenty species in three days."

He fielded questions as long as anyone would ask them, and then, trying to keep peoples' minds off the muggy, oppressive heat, he asked Zan to talk about CEDAM and underwater archaeology.

Zan did this with humor and verve, but it was getting hotter. Morgan volunteered some advice on taking bird photos. The bus was nearly a sauna. Mrs. Cunningham began to complain in shrill tones and Mrs. Bowdrie lay with her head back, as if nearly prostrated.

Tory whispered in Mildred's ear, "Why not teach them the song now? Then we can all sing at the party."

"But I don't have my guitar," Mildred protested.

"We don't have air-conditioning, either. Do it, Mildred! It'll take everyone back to their school days."

"We-e-ell," said Mildred reluctantly, "I will if you'll help."

Tory started to say she couldn't sing, but that was cheating, after urging Mildred to perform. "Let's go," she said, and stood back for Mildred to precede her up the aisle.

~ IX ~

The bird and animal choruses had everyone cooing or screeching, barking or mewling, and they demanded repeats till they knew the words. There was a round of applause as Mildred and Tory went back to their seats and Morgan slid out to let Tory resume her place by Brandy.

"That reminds me of a camp song." Hal chuckled. "Remember that one about the music teacher, Frieda?"

She did. The Callahans, curly redheads moving in rhythm, led a long build-on song with motions, about a professor who could play everything from bagpipes to violins. When they sat down, Gaye Burns remembered a comic flower song and Etheridge Martin came in with Boston sea chanties.

Tory had been singing when she knew the words and humming when she didn't, but as gray-haired Etheridge sat down amid clapping, she saw that Brandy didn't join in.

"Don't you feel well?" she asked in concern.

"It's astounding to see intelligent adults regress to Boy Scouts and Campfire Girls."

"At times like this, it helps," said Tory after a dumbfounded moment.

"Perhaps." Brandy sighed. "But did you really have to egg on Miss Halliday? Sing-along in Spanish with hoots and howls for the chorus!"

"Everyone but you seemed to like it. Even the Bowdries joined in and Mrs. Cunningham laughed."

Brandy shrugged. "As I said, either from heat or hysteria, the group seem to have gone back to their adolescences, a process I find undesirable and impossible." He smiled and the frigidity left his tone. "Maybe my problem is that I keep thinking how good it would be to have carried you off. We'd have been in Mérida by now instead of this steambath."

"I'm sorry you're not enjoying the trip," Tory said. "But I am." Somewhat defiantly, she joined in the German drinking songs that Mark Summerville was calling out. Brandy, with a doggedly patient expression, returned to his portfolio.

The countryside had gentle green valleys and forested hills. There were some cattle and more of handsome horses that were the size of ponies but able to carry men. Late in the afternoon, Dina turned off the main road and bumped down a dirt one, halting among a scattering of small white lodges and thatched open shelters.

"Here we are," said Theron. "The restaurant-bar is that biggest thatched structure just ahead and they'll have our meal ready at seven. I'll be out in half an hour if anyone cares to bird a little."

Two boys of eleven or twelve seemed to be the motel's sole representatives so, as Theron handed out keys, most people who could manage their luggage did. Brandy started to take Elspeth's and Tory's gear, but Zan scooped it up.

"You're in one of the bungalows over yonder," he told Brandy. "Why don't you go ahead and I'll settle the ladies? It seems the motel's out of rooms, and as the latecomer I get a hammock in the office."

Brandy eyed the distant bungalow and didn't argue. "Let's meet for cocktails before dinner," he said. "Thanks, Ericson."

Tory and Elspeth carried their small bags while Zan lugged the big ones, unlocked the door of one of the white double units, and stared about the tiny room in vain search of a place to put the bags and allow their owners room to step around.

"Dump them on the beds," Tory suggested. "Goodness, I think I'd prefer your hammock."

"I'll share." Zan grinned. "I'd better get out of here so you can maneuver. I'll tell the boys to bring you some ice. The tap water's supposed to be safe."

He exited to their thanks. Surveying the room, aunt and niece gave simultaneous groans and collapsed on the beds with their feet atop their luggage.

A small table between the two beds held a kerosene lamp in case of electric failure, one glass, and an earthenware cup. One rickety chair half-blocked the bathroom entrance, and a shelf holding two blankets had a bamboo rod attached to its underside, which sported two sadly bent and rusted hangers. On a stool by the door roosted a formidably large fan. The slatted door and the one window created a draft, but it was still overpoweringly hot and humid.

Tory got up and turned on the fan, filled the glass for Elspeth and the cup for herself. The bathroom was almost as large as the other room, but couldn't be utilized for hanging or storage because there was no shower curtain or rod to shield the rest of the room from splashing. The fixtures were a startling maroon and the two thin towels were mildewed. However, the large window above the sink had many sectional openings; on these Tory planned to hang her laundry.

"Hacienda Uxmal it's not," she said, proffering the water to her weary aunt. "However, we won't need to be here except to sleep. The big problem is where to put our clothes."

After unpacking their toiletries, they could wedge their small cases under the bed, and Tory insisted Elspeth's suitcase have the chair. She stowed her own hangup bag between the foot of her bed and the door, and they each hung up the skirt and dress they had allowed themselves.

There was a rap on the door. Avoiding the fan, Tory managed to open the door enough to admit the taller of the two boys, a shaggy-headed youngster with a broad white smile.

"Ice," he announced, depositing a clinking pitcher on the table. He made a sweeping gesture. "All okay?"

Tory hadn't the heart to complain, and besides, there was no use. This was clearly the only game in town.

"Okay, *gracias*," she said. "*¿Cómo se llama?*"

"Jorge, *señorita*." He smiled even more dazzlingly. "You need one thing, tell me, okay?"

"Okay." She shook his hand. "*Gracias*, Jorge."

Evading the fan and suitcase, he hurried out, and in a moment they heard him rap on the adjoining unit, which was inhabited by the Bowdries.

Tory yielded first shower to Elspeth and lay down to study up on birds of the area. She was concluding that it was going to be hard to tell the red-legged honeycreeper from the shining honeycreeper when there was another rap on the door.

Scrambling up, Tory found an excited Jorge clutching a note and an immense bouquet of orchids. "Don Luis!" he gasped. "Don Luis!"

"Who?" Tory frowned. Her mind clicked back. Zan had mentioned a wealthy Don Luis, his partner. Brandy seemed to have met him, too. Could this be the same man?

She took the note. "*Señorita muy estimada*," it began and to her relief, continued in English. "I have heard of you from my friend, Alexander Ericson. Please accept these flowers as a welcome to Palenque. I should be honored if you and your esteemed aunt would join Alexander and me for dinner. I have, of course, invited your fiancé, Mr. Sherrod."

"Minuto, por favor," Tory dazedly told Jorge. She put the magnificent purple flowers on the table, where they overhung the alarm clock and water pitcher, went to the curtained bathroom door, and passed the note in to Elspeth, who had finished showering and was getting dressed.

"Let's go," said Elspeth promptly. "We'll be cheek-by-jowling with our *compañeros* thrice daily for the next week."

"I'll leave it to Brandy, then."

Tory scribbled a note and asked Jorge to deliver it to Señor Sherrod. He bobbed his head, ducked the fan, and sped out. Apparently this Don Luis had an inspiring effect. Tory had her shower, sprayed on cologne to cover the scent of mildewed towel, and put on her terry robe. As she stepped out of the bath, which now looked as if it had endured a flood, Elspeth handed her a note.

"I let Jorge go on," she said. "He must have plenty to do besides play carrier pigeon."

"This won't need an answer," Tory said. "Brandy's delighted with the invitation. A car will pick us up about seven and take us to Don Luis' place."

The gray Rolls-Royce had Zan in front by the driver and Brandy came to the door for Tory and Elspeth. The driver, darkly good-looking and wearing a white *guayabera,* wished them a good evening and held the back door of the Rolls for Elspeth before he rushed around to let Tory enter on the opposite side.

Brandy wore a silver-gray raw-silk suit that emphasized his eyes and hair. Zan had no coat, but his white cotton shirt had piratically full sleeves and its slash throat revealed the shining black pendant he'd been wearing the day she met him. His skin was very brown and his eyes shone green.

"I'm proud to present such lovely countrywomen to my partner," he said. "Don Luis will lose his heart at first glance."

Brandy looked approvingly at Tory's super-best and, for this tour, only dress, clinging violet blue with push-up long sleeves, deep-scooped neck revealing the *Matanceros* madonna, and wide draping sash. The humidity had given her hair a draggled look, but she'd fastened it up with a blue chiffon scarf and Elspeth had assured her the effect was nice. Elspeth wore a dusty green dress of India cotton patterned with tiny mirrors and embroidery. It set off her remarkable complexion and fluffy white hair to such advantage that Tory wished Theron could see her.

"Let's hope," said Brandy, as they jounced over the dirt road and slipped with a final jar onto the highway, "that my presence will help Don Luis keep his heart—and head. Does he spend much time here?"

"As much as at any place, I'd reckon," said Zan. "He's interested in the restorations at Palenque and he hunts. Yucatán lives up to its old name, Land of the Deer and the Pheasant. Not to mention jaguars."

"Jaguars," repeated Elspeth.

"They're not very big," consoled Zan. "And they're shy. But you can meet them occasionally walking down a jungle trail after a rain."

The driver turned up a side road that gradually climbed a hill by winding around it on a road hidden from below by dense trees. Twilight was thickening and the beam of their headlights glinted off glossy green leaves or picked out the strange dark-red bark of the gumbo limbo or *indio desnudo*, naked Indian. At last the Rolls passed through a gate opened by an old man and approached a white stone house with graceful Moorish arches facing the circular drive, surrounded by an ivy-grown rock border and a profusion of flowers.

Stopping by the central arch, the driver let Elspeth out, but Brandy climbed out on his side and gave Tory a steadying hand.

She straightened to gaze into tawny lion eyes that widened in admiration and—was it calculation? *"Encantado."* The strongly built rather stocky man bowed. His thick wild hair was golden-brown and he wore a white *guayabera* exquisitely embroidered in white, white slacks, and sandals.

Zan made introductions which Don Luis acknowledged with great charm, telling Brandy how much he valued the Til Riemenschneider Mary Magdalene Brandy had located for him.

"Riemenschneider was a German master carver," Brandy explained. "During the Peasants' Rebellion, while Martin Luther was saying the poor should be suppressed, Riemenschneider sym-

pathized with them so the Prince-Bishop of Würz-
burg maimed his hands. He carved no more. Pity
he didn't stick to his work."

"I don't think it's a pity at all," said Tory. "The
pity is what the bishop did."

"At least we can agree that Riemenschneider is
remembered and his art admired every day, while
no one remembers that prince-bishop except for
the atrocity," Don Luis put in.

The arched veranda ran the length of the building, red-brown tile polished to a sheen, planters
and pots of flowers enough to beautify without
overwhelming. Carved settees, chairs, and tables
broke the expanse. In addition to the large arched
door through which their host led them, two
smaller arches gave access to the main building.

Hacienda Uxmal had prepared Tory for an experience of vast stretches of tile, many arches, and
high ceilings, but it was after all a hotel expanded
to house many guests. Don Luis' house was much
smaller, but its scale was similar. The room in
which they stood must have been a hundred feet
long and half that in width with a beehive-shaped
fireplace in the center, its space filled now with
scarlet flowers. Velvet couches and chairs in muted
greens and rusts surrounded the fireplace interspersed with heavy carved octagonal tables inset
with copper and tile.

Other seating groups were clustered throughout
the room, which was lit by three tremendous ham-
mered copper chandeliers. The walls were an art
gallery, Riveras and Orozcos and others Tory

couldn't identify. In niches set in the wall near the ceiling a whole multitude of madonnas looked down, some smiling, some grieving, some in sumptous robes and crowns, others in simple blue or white, some enthroned on the crescent moon, others amid flowers. There was even a life-size copy of the little sea virgin of the *Mantanceros*.

Tory caught her breath in delight, hand going involuntarily to her throat. Don Luis smiled at her. "So you have seen that one?"

"At Akumal. She's very lovely, looking out to sea."

"Then you must have this one to remind you to return," said Don Luis.

"Oh, no!" demurred Tory, horrified.

"Do not deny me the pleasure." Don Luis glanced at Brandy. "Señor Sherrod, you permit the gift?"

"Of course." Brandy pressed Tory's hand warningly. "You're very kind."

"Selfish." Don Luis laughed, giving an order to a hovering servant. "I wish to ensure that the *señorita* will now and then be compelled to remember me."

Tory blushed furiously at this extravagance. He didn't mean a word of it, but she had no techniques for gracefully dealing with such gallant banter, felt gauche and tongue-tied. She was to have no respite, either, for as soon as he had brought them through a smaller veranda into a courtyard garden surrounded on three sides by the U shape of the house, Don Luis placed himself between her and Elspeth at a round wrought-iron and marble table near a fountain where an onyx jaguar threatened a jade serpent in a grotto above a waterfall. Blue and green light beamed from the fountain and other lights glowed softly from trees and vines. A copper lantern lit the table, and two white-clad attendants took drink requests and mixed them at a small bar on the rear veranda.

"You got your flowers?" Don Luis asked Tory.

"They're marvelous!" Tory didn't add that they also took up all the room on their single table. "Thank you very much."

"Thank you for giving the flowers the happy fate of sharing the air you breathe."

Tory took a long draught of that. "Don Luis," she said forthrightly, "your compliments are flattering, but I don't know what to say to them."

Zan chuckled and so did Don Luis. "It's not necessary to reply, enchanting lady. Smile if my poor efforts please you and accept them as your due."

"But they're not," Tory said flatly. "They make me uncomfortable. I know you belong to CEDAM and have a great interest in your country's history and art. Please, Don Luis, can't we talk about those things?"

Glass halted halfway to his lips, he stared at her with golden eyes that seemed to dilate. Beyond him, Brandy looked absolutely stricken and Zan astounded, though his lips twitched.

"Tory," Elspeth chided. "How rude!"

Slowly, Don Luis reached for Tory's hand, raised it to his lips with his irresistibly strong fingers. "I cry pardon for my nonsense, which was meant to amuse you, *señorita*." Good-humored irony veined his tone. "What especially would you like to talk about?"

Discomfited, Tory glanced around for help. "I'd like to hear more about the *Mantanceros*," Brandy said.

Don Luis and Zan told of salvaging not only from the *Matanceros,* but from *La Nicolasa,* one of the conqueror Montejo's ships, and from the wrecks of the *Cañizares* and the *Paletas.* This occupied them through a most delicious lemon-flavored chicken soup; deer *zik,* which Don Luis explained was shredded roast venison mixed with chopped onions, radishes, *serrano* peppers, coriander, and the juice of bitter oranges; and a main course of cochinita pibil, roast pig slowly roasted in a dressing of *achiote* and bitter orange mixed with, again according to Don Luis, Tabasco peppers, oregano, black pepper, mint, onions, salt, and pork rind.

There were Mayan tamales called *dtzotobichay,* and when Tory flavored hers with a bit of in-nocuous-looking sauce, her tongue burned and her eyes watered.

"Now you know why we call that *ixni-pec,* or dog nose," consoled Don Luis. "The *habanero chile* turns any nose as moist as that of a healthy dog."

Tory nodded heartfelt agreement, separated her tamale from the sauce, and proceeded to enjoy it while Brandy turned the conversation back to the *Matanceros,* which seemed to especially fascinate him.

"Has anyone ever looked for those chests of salvaged treasure?" he demanded.

Don Luis shrugged. "Men always hunt any known buried treasure, but if the *Matanceros* chests have been found or smuggled out of Mexico, I've heard nothing of it. Have you, Zan?"

Zan shook his head. "Probably easier for looters to find a *stele* and saw it up or steal from unprotected sites. The jungles have probably swallowed more ruins than the ones that are recognized and Mexico hasn't the money to protect all its antiquities."

Dessert was chilled fresh fruit and velvety almond liqueur. Don Luis rose, suggesting coffee in the library. This proved to be adjoining the main hall. Tory noticed that the *Matanceros* madonna was already gone, felt embarrassed as Don Luis caught her glance.

"With permission, I will send it to your Mérida hotel," he said with a twinkle. "Even fervently admired things can get in the way on a journey."

Tory thanked him, but with a growing resentment, aware that she had needed to thank him all evening long. He had done too much for her comfort. She was casting about for some way of repaying him at least a little when they stepped into the library and her problems were solved.

Thousands of volumes filled the shelves, lay open on stands, or were on tables by various easy chairs. "Why do you heave such a relieved sigh?" asked Don Luis behind her. "Did you think me a Bluebeard with his wives hid away in jars?"

"I'm glad to see you love books. You have a fabulous collection, but I've never known a book-lover who didn't want more."

"Books rank with my love for the sea," he admitted. "But you don't smile now. What is it?"

Tory looked away from the alcove surrounding a huge desk. The walls were hung with hides and horns.

"They distress you?" he asked softly enough that no one overheard. Her face was apparently answer enough. "It's musty in here," he announced. "Let's have coffee on the terrace."

"The hunting must be good," said Brandy as they moved out to the main veranda. "Were those spotted hides jaguar?"

Don Luis nodded. "And there are puma and white-lipped peccary. Probably the most difficult quarry is the brocket deer. They're a rust color and no taller than a large dog, blend right into the thickets. Quantities of white-tail deer, of course, and ocellated turkey. You hunt, Don Brandon?"

"Not much. But I wouldn't mind having a crack at something really rare or hard to get."

"Well, if you fancy unusual game birds, there's the crested guan and the curassow."

"Not while you're on a bird tour." Tory re-coiled.

"Of course not," Brandy told her soothingly. "But I'd really like a jaguar hide."

The spotted skins had looked pathetically small to Tory, but this was not the place to try to change Brandy's mind. "It would be my pleasure to arrange a hunt," Don Luis said with an apologetic look at Tory. "However, you would have needed to get a consular certificate before you left the states, cleared your guns at a military installation, and got your license at a game warden's office."

"I have," said Brandy.

Gone through all those elaborate procedures and never said a word? Tory's jaw dropped before she clamped it shut. She didn't believe that engaged or even married people should bare to each other everything they did, but this was more like deliberate concealment.

"I brought a twelve-gauge shotgun, twenty-two and thirty-thirty rifles, a twenty-two caliber pistol, and all the allowed cartridges."

"That's four hundred cartridges." Zan whistled. "You should have gone on a safari, not a bird-watching trip."

"Don Brandon anticipates losing a lot of shots in the brush." Though Don Luis was smiling, there was a hard ring to his voice. "Yucatán has lots of game. We are glad to share it with sportsmen, but only an infantile mind can glory in bagging a hundred ducks in one day as some *norteameri-*

canos do or taking the same number of bonefish. Mexico lacks the money and men for enforcement, and the regrettable truth is that *norteamericanos* rate as perhaps the worst threat to conservation in Mexico."

"I will, of course, be completely guided by you," Brandy assured his host.

"Excellent! I have a Lacandon guide who knows every trail in this region." He laughed. "If you'd rather hunt with guns than binoculars, we could stay out several days, get back where only the Lacandones go."

"Superlative!" Brandy's eyes shone silver as the small goblets Don Luis now filled with brandy. "What a lucky chance to meet you again, Don Luis."

"Chance is a misunderstood and underrated deity," Don Luis said. His amber eyes swung to Tory so swiftly that it had the physical effect of a pounce. "I suppose, *señorita*, that hunting has no charms for you?"

In spite of her resolve to keep still till she could talk with Brandy alone, Tory couldn't refrain from saying in a voice that thrummed with angry frustration and repressed tears, "I loathe hunting."

Was that a glint of triumph or relief in his lazy stare? "I feared so," he murmured. "Do you go with us, Zan?"

"I'm bird-watching." Zan shrugged.

Don Luis raised an eyebrow. "But it is, I believe, a peculiarity of yours that you do not hunt?"

"I fish."

"And of course," said Brandy in a genial but somehow biting way, "your sudden but intense fascination with birds would preclude any turning aside."

"Just so." Zan nodded.

"Zan does hunt, though," mused Don Luis. "That black coral around his neck is only found in the depths. Few divers can bring it up. And he was among the first to notice the sleeping sharks off Cozumel."

"Sleeping sharks?" cried Tory and her aunt in unison.

"So called," said Zan. "Interesting beasties— or place, rather, sort of a garage for sharks. When they enter this sort of grotto, they seem to be asleep, lose their aggressiveness. And the little scavengers that pry parasites off them seem to be able to work much faster. One theory is that there's an unusual amount of oxygen in this spot, but whatever it is, the sharks come out after a few hours all tuned up and cleaned off and soon revert to their usual snappish disposition."

"They're taking tourists down to see them now," said Don Luis. "Though I can't think it's a good idea."

"I won't take anyone but qualified divers and damn few of them," said Zan.

Don Luis smiled gently. "Maybe we should check into it, Zan. Might be quite a money-maker."

Brandy laughed, a sweeping gesture of his hand indicating the incredible house and grounds.

"Money can't be much of a problem for you, Don Luis."

"The more one has, the more it costs to keep it all up," said Don Luis. "I'm always interested, as Zan will tell you, in ways to make pesos."

"True," said Zan. "Otherwise I wouldn't need a bookkeeper."

Tory started to tell him what he needed was a bilingual assistant or to run the shop himself, but bit off the dart when she remembered his partner was there.

"You go to the ruins tomorrow?" asked Don Luis. "I think them the most beautiful in Mexico."

They stayed on the safe subject of ruins till Aunt Elspeth glanced at her watch with a regretful sigh. "Six-o'clock birdwalks *do* make for early hours. But it's been an evening we'll never forget, Don Luis. Thank you for having us."

"A memorable pleasure," said Don Luis. They all got to their feet, and he gazed down at Tory with an amused curiosity that made her sure he enjoyed stalking more than animals. "I hope to see you before your stay is up."

"There's a party tomorrow night," remembered Elspeth. "The entertainment will be strictly amateur, but you're very welcome."

"If you ladies will be there," said Don Luis grandiloquently, "no other diversion could tempt me. I will assuredly come."

He sent for the car and kissed Elspeth's and Tory's hands before installing his guests in the luxurious depths of the Rolls.

"Hasta luego," he called as they drove away.

Aunt Elspeth sighed and leaned back on the opulent cushioning. "What a man! If I were twenty years younger . . ." She chuckled philosophically. "Oh, well, as it is, I can have the fun with none of the danger. If I were you, Tory, I'd not dance off in the shadows. Or maybe I would!"

Tory didn't respond. Without the distraction of Don Luis' engrossing remarks about the ruins, she came back to brood on Brandy's possession of the guns, his going to considerable trouble to prepare for a hunt without breathing a hint to her. It shook her badly, not the hunting so much as his secretiveness.

They would have to talk about it. She dreaded the prospect; a disagreement with Brandy knotted her stomach before and after, made her physically wretched. But this had opened a gulf between them that widened the more she thought about it. It was like watching a hidden crevice in the ground swell till it could no longer be ignored, but have no way of telling how deep and long it was.

As the chauffeur stopped at their motel, Tory gulped and blurted in a strangled way, "Brandy, will—will you get out here and stay awhile? I need to talk with you."

"Oh, my love," groaned Brandy. "I'm dead tired. Won't it wait?"

Something clicked in Tory. He didn't seem at all distressed about having covered his hunting intentions from her, or in the least eager to have it clean and clear between them. "It'll wait," she said. "If you're so exhausted, please don't see us to the door."

"Nonsense, darling." Helping her out while the chauffeur assisted her aunt, he slipped her hand and arm possessively through his. "I'll take my scolding tomorrow," he promised after Elspeth had gone in. "But sleep on it first, my sweetheart. Things always bulk larger at night. It's the time for looming shadows and poor perspective."

She refused to be cajoled into a smile. "Good night."

He drew her abruptly around. "Not like that," he whispered. His mouth claimed hers. He held her closer than he ever had. His lips grew compelling, ruthless. But, for once, Tory wasn't stirred. She didn't fight him, there would be no use, but she felt as if she observed the kiss from outside herself.

At last he drew away, eyes like frozen flame. "You're worn out, poor child. Sleep well and I'll see you at breakfast."

She stepped inside, avoiding the fan. The Rolls pulled away and rolled back past in five minutes. "Aren't you coming to bed?" Elspeth called.

"I'm too keyed up. Think I'll stroll around awhile."

"Don't leave the road and the hamlet. We don't want jaguars to get you even if they do have pretty spotted skins."

"I don't think it's funny," Tory said with violence.

Elspeth sighed. "Nor do I. But don't stay up all night over it."

"I'll just walk a bit. Go to sleep, dear. I'll be careful. And I'll lock the door so the jaguars won't get you."

"More likely to be eaten by mosquitoes. They're buzzing like mad."

"The repellent's under the orchids on your side," Tory said, and went back out into the languorous scented night.

~ XI ~

Though the motel rooms left much to be desired,
the little complex itself was fascinating. Scattered
among the motel units and private dwellings were
several thatched open shelters with tables, and
great trees reached up to the road. The restaurant-
bar was dark now, but as Tory wandered into a
clearing where grass was lush beneath her feet,
the late moon glowed on the white stone features
of an uptilted Mayan head resting amid boulders
from which a fountain splashed in soft music.
Flowering vines hung low about it from the single
tree in that small park. She sat on a bench where
she could watch and hear the crystalline water.

Natural beauty usually acted on her like balm,
but tonight it could not. She and Brandy had never
discussed hunting, but he'd almost certainly
guessed her attitude. She wouldn't have tried to
persuade him to give up something important to
him, but she would—and did—have to consider if
she could live with a man who killed for sport or
trophies.

Even more troubling was his failure to mention

what must have been time-consuming preparations. That must have been why he'd gone down to Nuevo Laredo the week before they left, to get his hunting license, but he'd only said it was business.

Maybe that was Brandy's attitude, that only their joint life concerned her, but Tory rejected that sort of compartmentalized relationship. She didn't want to marry a man who'd hide aspects of his life from her.

So could she marry Brandy?

A spasm of pain twisted through her. The peaceful moonlit face of the Maya blurred and she blinked back tears. No use going over it again and again. They'd talk it out tomorrow. Why couldn't she remember instead what a wonderful evening it had been in every other way? From the time the orchids arrived, it had been like an enchantment, though the magical house was ruled by virile, handsome Don Luis, not a beast or monster of fairy tales.

He talked such gallant extravagance that there was no danger of taking it seriously. Still, it was extraordinarily kind of him to give her the *Matanceros* madonna copy. Foolish to attach undue importance to that, though, when he was taking Brandy on a hunt that would require considerable expense and preparation.

Back to Brandy and his at-least-tacit deception.

Tory felt like walking over to his bungalow and demanding that he talk the whole thing out that night. She would have if she could have believed she could wake him without disturbing his neighbors and alerting the group that the tour's single romance was in rough waters. Tory heaved an exasperated sigh.

If she forced Brandy to come out, he'd be angry, and since she already was, it was a poor time to try to settle an issue that could break their plans for marriage, wreck what had seemed such a happy future.

There might be some perfectly good reason why he'd forgotten to tell her about the license and guns. Better try to put it out of mind and get to sleep.

Turning, Tory collided with a tall solid figure. She recoiled, a startled cry rising to her lips, to be stifled by a hard mouth that seemed to demand and plead at the same time. Resisting the treacherous response of her racing blood, a sweet dizzying light-headedness that robbed her of strength, Tory summoned all her strength, mental and physical, and pulled free of Zan.

"What are you doing, creeping up on people like that?" She choked.

"You're not *people*, you're *you*, singular." Tory burned at the laughter in his voice. "Very singular," he continued genially. "And I didn't creep, exactly. I've been standing here five minutes waiting for you to come out of your trance. Don Luis affect you that profoundly?"

"Don Luis is a gracious host and a prodigious flatterer."

Zan's eyebrow arched wickedly. "What cynicism! Dare I ask then what you were thinking and heaving sighs about?"

"It's none of your business, Alexander Ericson Grande." She started past him, but he caught her wrists, held them in a deceptively gentle clasp that she knew could tighten to steel.

"Let's take a little walk," he suggested. "Where we won't be overheard or interrupted."

"I—I'm tired!"

"Yes, but we both know you're too mad to go to sleep right now, so why not have a stroll in the moonlight and exercise—pardon me—exorcise your spleen?"

Because it is moonlight and the air's sweet and sensuous and heady and you just kissed me and your hands turn me weak.

"I don't think talking to you will soothe me in the least. As for strolling, I want to make that six-o'clock birdwalk and it's getting late."

"Early. One in the morning." As she glared at him, sensing that an effort to escape would bring indignities, he smiled, coaxingly. "You're wide awake and you know it, Tory. Give me ten minutes."

"All right," she grudged. "I suppose it's the only way to get rid of you, short of shrieking like a banshee."

"Wrong country, honey. Here it would be La Llorona, the Weeping One. Never mind," he added kindly in a tone that made her want to gnash her teeth. "It's the thought that counts."

"What," she demanded frostily as they reached

the drive and moved down it past the widely dispersed buildings, "do you want to talk about?"

He shrugged. "I thought you might need to let off steam. You weren't happy with your fiancé when he wouldn't stay for a little question-and-answer session."

Tory bit her lip. "With your talent for jumping to conclusions, you should train for the Olympics."

His fingers tightened on her arm. His voice held a similar heightened tension. "Did you really not know he'd brought in guns and had a license?"

"I never even knew he hunted," Tory blurted.

"Sounds like you don't know your prospective husband very well. I'm surprised at you, Victoria. You've certainly been suspicious enough of me, and poor Don Luis gets speedily indexed under L for Latin lover."

"I didn't have Brandy fill in a questionnaire or take a lie-detector test," she disdained. "What good's a marriage if you're that distrustful?"

"Exactly."

She was glad the moonlight hid her long slow blush. "I can't see that any of this is your concern."

He stopped walking. "Can't you?" he asked after a moment during which she could not look up.

"No."

He dropped her hands, walked briskly on, and though she could have escaped now, she didn't. "I happen to think people should know the people they marry," he said. "And either you're a clever actress or you don't know Brandon Sherrod."

"And you do?"

"I'm finding out. What was he doing at that isolated ruin at Uxmal the day Perrito killed the snake?"

"Why, he went walking. Why not?"

"He hasn't shown much enthusiasm for the scheduled walks. Didn't it seem funny that he suddenly got energetic?"

"Not any stranger than your suddenly joining up with the tour. I can't believe that you couldn't have learned by yourself about all you really care to know about birds."

His voice was amused. "You know perfectly well, Tory, that I wasn't about to let you get away."

Her heart leaped, but she sternly commanded it to behave. "Yes, that's why you stayed up till all hours with Morgan Scott."

"Am I supposed to stare at you and Brandy like a kid without a dime passing an ice-cream place on an August day?"

She shook her head impatiently. "You didn't come along because of me. It's something else! What is it, Zan?"

"Ah, so now you're asking questions?"

"Yes. Why are you so interested in Brandy?"

"He's your fiancé."

"That's not it."

Zan laughed. "Looks like we'll just both have to wonder, doesn't it?" He swung around. "If we're making that early birdwalk, we'd better tuck in."

They walked back to her room in a silence electric with feelings and thoughts that Tory at least was determined not to express. She was sure now that something was going on.

What? It might be flattering to believe Zan had come on the tour because of her, but she didn't. And Don Luis. He seemed a shrewd playboy, but had he just happened to be near Palenque or was he involved in the mystification?

It was like trying to pick your way through a dark room without tripping over things you knew must be there but of which you had no conception of their shape, size, location, or menace.

"Good night," Zan said at the door. He didn't try to kiss her, but turned away into the night.

Feeling oddly let down, Tory moved cautiously past the humming fan, but in spite of her physical weariness, it was a long time before she slept. She had to talk with Brandy. There might be an easy answer to it all. But she had to have an answer.

Tory pushed in the screeching alarm. As she and her aunt edged past each other, Elspeth yawned and got in a corner to brush her hair.

"Not room enough to change your mind," she said. "But the mattress is all right."

"And the shower works, not wisely but too well." Tory grinned, perching on the end of the bed to tie her shoelaces.

They joined the others in the road. Brandy wasn't there and Morgan was busy showing Zan how her telephoto lens worked.

Tory dutifully raised her binoculars when a bird was sighted, but she doubted she would ever know one woodcreeper from another, and except for the striped-headed kiskadees, she couldn't distinguish between most of the flycatchers. Dispiriting. But there was a gorgeous blue-tailed hummingbird, a pretty little rufous-tailed jacamar, and a schoolmasterishly handsome Amazon kingfisher who looked as if he were wearing a high starched white collar.

Giant trees—mahogany, several kinds of *sapote*, cedar, and gumbo-limbo—reared above smaller trees, and golden cassia brightened the green depths of the forest. The moist air was heavy with odors of earth, mold, and flowers.

Theron kept the walk short so they could breakfast and get an early start to the ruins. Tory went to the motel to freshen up, and as she came down the road to the restaurant, a small salt-and-pepper bristled animal with small neat hooves advanced on her.

It resembled a miniature wild boar and Tory knew it must be a peccary, or *jabalí*. That these were found in her home state didn't cheer her much. They were known to be vicious when cornered. She wasn't trying to corner this one, but it seemed to have designs on her. Tory was looking around for a tree when Narciso ambled around the bus and bent down to scratch the animal between its pointed ears.

"Petunia," he said to Tory. And he raised the long straight mouth, signaling the tusks were gone. "Not hurt you, *señorita*. Friend."

"Mmmm—*sí*."

Petunia affably followed them to the open-sided restaurant, where she was regarded with such fear and loathing by Mrs. Cunningham and Etheridge Martin that Narciso got some scraps from the kitchen and lured her away. Four or five assorted dogs roved under and between the tables, and a jumble of cats paraded about the periphery. The tablecloths were clean, though, and the coffee was hot and aromatic.

Brandy had saved a place for Tory. When Narciso returned from decoying Petunia, there were no vacant seats except for one between Tory and Morgan. Tory waved him over in spite of Brandy's displeased look. Tory didn't care. What she had to say to her fiancé needed privacy; till that chance came, she preferred as little conversation as possible.

Trying to think of something to ask Narciso, she remembered Mildred's voiceless Mayan dogs and decided to try to find out if they had descendants.

"Narciso," she began as a stocky rather desperate-looking waiter presented them with plates of eggs scrambled with chilis and dollops of refried beans. *"Los perros de los Mayas antiguos no tienen"*—she paused and tried to think of a word that might mean bark—*"ruido?"* she asked hopefully. *"¿Voz?"* He stared, blinking. Tory could think of nothing else. Brandy was frowning. That made her more determined to get across her meaning. *"Los perros no tienen . . . woof-woof,"* she said. *"¿Sabe? Woof-woof?"*

Narciso gaped, then lowered his head, shook with laughter. Brandy's frown deepened to a scowl. "Victoria, for heaven's sake!"

Tory ignored him. "Narciso," she insisted, "*¿tienen los perros modernos de Yucatán woof-woof?*"

Again convulsions. When he could speak, he nodded. "Dogs have woof-woof—*ladrido.*"

"*¡Quá lástima!*" she said, conscious of Brandy's outrage, though she kept her back to him. She called down the table to Mildred. "There aren't any more of those barkless dogs."

"Then we'll dedicate our song to them," Mildred proposed.

"Wonderful."

"What are you talking about?" Brandy whispered.

"Our number for the party tonight." Tory gave him an innocent smile. "What are you doing?"

"I think I'd better stay away and avoid the sight of you making a fool of yourself."

Tory stiffened.

"I'm sorry," he said at once, patting her hand. "But I can't understand why a tour should regress everyone to summer-camp mentality."

"It seemed to inspire you to become a Great White Hunter!" Tory bit her lip. Mustn't get into that in front of people. "When will we have a chance to talk, Brandy? Are you going on the ruins trip?"

"I've got things to take care of in case Don Luis

does get our trip organized by tomorrow. But why not after lunch?"

Though she was annoyed with him for once more defaulting as a member of the tour, she was relieved not to have to go around the ruins with him pretending nothing was wrong.

"I'll see you then," she said, and hurried with her breakfast because Theron was waving his wristwatch aloft.

∼❮ XII ❯∼

Surrounded by great trees and blossoming vines, the ruins of Palenque spread along the top of a high hill, gleaming white in the morning sun. Theron spotted their first toucans as they approached the Temple of the Inscriptions and these yellow-cheeked and -breasted birds with scarlet undertail coverts and immense curving green and orange bills had to be admired before even Beata could be lured to the ruins.

An official guide met them at the bottom of the steps of the temple and led them to the porticoed building on top. From here they descended steep stone stairs going far down in air that grew thick and clammy as that of the Cave of Balankanche. The way was packed both going and coming as Tory saw when she glanced back to see if she could retreat.

"Courage," murmured Zan in her ear. She had last seen him comparing toucans with Morgan and scolded herself for feeling so absurdly glad that he was near her.

At last it was her turn to peer through a glass

into the crypt of a priest-king who had been buried in jade jewels and a jade mask over 1,200 years before. A handsomely carved slab covered the burial.

The Lord Pacal still slept in his city, though the jungle had repossessed much of it and jaguars and serpents dwelled in the overgrown rubble of what had been the holy city. It had covered five miles, but the reclaimed part was only five hundred yards long and three hundred wide.

Tory's clothes stuck to her by the time she reached the upper air. She moved at once to the pillars surrounding the crypt entrance, where Beata was telling the bewildered guide why Palenque had fallen into decay so that when the Spaniards came only a few groups of Indians lived in the area.

"The soil was becoming less fertile at the same time it was being expected to produce enough surplus to feed and give luxurious lives to the aristocrats and priests. As long as this group seemed worth supporting because they provided closer ties to the gods and brought prosperity, the system worked, but drought and famine destroy a ruling class's potency if no remedy can be found. The workers probably just faded away into the jungles to eke out their living without being encumbered by the expensive upkeep of priests and nobles, or they drove these out or massacred them."

"Upper classes can't exist without a foundation," said Hal Callahan. He gazed across at the palace and the various temples spreading to where a forested knoll rose above them. "How strange it must have been if the priests were left with their gods and no people."

"It happened all over," Beata said. "The great ceremonial cities were deserted before the Spaniards came and only vestiges of Mayan culture remained."

The guide cleared his throat, reassuming control of the assembling group. "There were wars, too," he said. "Uxmal, Chichén Itzá, and Mayapán fought and weakened each other, but at Palenque we do not think there was war. Now we go to the palace."

Zan fell in step with Tory. He spoke whimsically. "Do you suppose it matters to the gods that instead of sacrifices here they're offered tamales and corn gruel and *balché*, the native beer, back in Lacandon villages?"

"Really?"

"Sure. Instead of temples and altars, little god pots, made new each year, receive *balché*, incense, and food, and the small image in each pot is supposed to take the offerings and prayers to the real god. It's much folksier."

Brandy would want some of those pots if he found out about them. Tory sighed. She'd never thought of it in Texas, but being linked with a collector of rarities had distinctly unpleasant possibilities.

Supposing he wanted something that belonged to someone else or something forbidden? She could see him now, barging into an Indian settlement and trying to carry off what were, after all, the mystical abodes of the spirits of their gods. Don Luis, thank goodness, was a forceful man himself and should be able to check Brandy if anyone could.

The poor guide had a frustrating time herding his binocular-addicted charges to the huge platform where several buildings rose to dominate the center of the site. The four-storied tower had probably been an observatory. There were some very fine large bas-reliefs in the interior patio, and the guide pointed out an ingenious stone latrine. Inside the building facing the steps leading to the ground from the three-hundred foot-long top of the platform, the guide showed where archaeologists were reconstructing parts of the frieze and then brought them to a wall where even the most avid birder stopped squinting for wings and gazed in wonder.

"Here is Pacal receiving the emblems of kingship from his mother," said the guide, pleased to have found something at last to rivet them. "She had been regent and always exercised much influence with him. He came to power when he was twelve years and 125 days old. He married his sister and may have at least ceremonially wed his mother, Lady Zac-Kuk."

"Shocking," muttered Mrs. Cunningham.

"Perfectly sensible way of keeping the royal bloodlines straight," said Beata. "Goes back to the Egyptians."

The guide gestured toward the northern group

of structures and the temples in the southeastern edge of the clearing beyond the canal. "Much more to see. Not much I can tell you. Good-bye!"

Theron lingered to pay and thank him after calling out that the bus would leave the parking lot at 12:30 sharp and that meanwhile he was going to look for birds around the northern group because no other tourists would be wandering up there.

"I shall visit the temples," Beata said, managing to look regal in spite of a sunburned nose and floppy blue sun hat. She cast Mrs. Cunningham's shoulders an annoyed look. "Quite impossible to be attuned to forces and magnetisms if the atmosphere is contaminated with alien vibrations. Will you come with me, Tory?"

Tory thought Beata was being rather harsh, but she, too, preferred browsing around in quiet. "Yes, let's do go," she said.

So while the main group went north with Theron, she and Beata walked along the path to the Sun Temple, so identified by Beata, who had bought and studied some scholarly works on the site. The small platform housed an open-fronted shrine, the wall portraying two priests standing on the backs of kneeling slaves while they made offerings to the sun, portrayed as a rather greedy-looking, almost square object supported on a dais held by more kneeling figures.

"The sun shone on the panel," Beata explained. "From here you can look straight to the Temple of

the Foliated Cross, which must have received the
last rays of the setting sun."

They detoured briefly to what Beata said was
the tomb of Pacal's wife, a woman wearing a sym-
bol resembling the Egyptian *ankh,* or key of life.
From this they passed the Temple of the Cross to
treacherous remnants of steps leading up to the
temple with its ornate friezed top.

The inner shrine showed a cross embellished
with maize leaves and human heads. "Pacal is
offering a sacramental bloodletter to the cross,"
said Beata. "And that's his son, Chan-Bahlum,
holding a perforator to show he'll go on carrying
out the ritual self-mutilation."

Tory shuddered. "I'd never have guessed!
Those things they're holding look like some sort of
weird musical instruments."

"No. They were used to pierce an ear or tongue
or other part of the body to make a blood offering.
It had to do with increasing the fertility of the
land. Blood sacrifice is a very old idea." Beata
smiled forgivingly at Tory's revulsion, glanced at
her watch. "Oh, dear! I'm going to skip the Temple
of the Cross because there's just time for the
museum. Which will you do?"

"The temple," decided Tory.

Beata's interest in blood had made Tory think
she might be just as happy, though not so well-
informed, if she roamed by herself. They gingerly
descended. Beata hurried off toward the museum
and Tory threaded her way over crumbling stones
and sand to the largest of the three southern

temples. It was considerably taller than the other two and gave a splended view toward the palace and Temple of the Inscriptions.

Turning from this delight, Tory surveyed the carved slabs flanking the door of the shrine and was relieved that here Pacal, if it was he, held a pipe from which came clouds of either music or smoke. He wore a jaguar skin and a fantastic bird head-dress.

"You look like a Mayan Pied Piper," she told him.

"Will you follow?" came a voice from inside the shrine.

Tory jumped, sprang back, then gritted her teeth as she recognized the man who stepped into the door. "Very funny!" she seethed. "What are you doing lurking about like that?"

"I brought an offering."

Tory snorted.

"It's true," he insisted in a wounded tone. "Look at the shrine."

Tory gazed past him. On the floor in front of another carving of Pacal and his son making offerings lay some of the red snapdragonlike flowers especially loved by hummingbirds.

"I don't think you'll get much in return for those," she sniffed.

"Oh, a blood offering went with it." He showed his scratched hands. "I had to reach through some brambles for them."

"I thought you went with the birders."

"Not when I saw you come this way."

Her pulse quickened in that ridiculous way it persisted in doing when Zan gave her more than a fleeting glance, but she was suspicious, too. "Are you shadowing me?" she demanded.

He leaned against the doorway, eyes probing deep though his tone was light. "What makes you say such a thing?"

"You turned up last night by the fountain. And at Uxmal when I took Perrito off to the little ruins you came out of the scenery almost as suddenly as that snake."

"I wonder how Perrito is?" he mused. "Hope he'll like going out in the boat."

"And you materialized this morning."

"I didn't intend to till you started talking to the carving. I was just going to let you wonder who'd put the flowers in the shrine and follow you from afar. But when you tried to chat with old jaguar-hide here I thought maybe you'd talk to me."

"You have a great talent for being where you're not expected."

He shrugged and laughed. "Expect me, then, and you won't be startled."

"It—it's like being trailed by a private eye."

"Say the word and I'll march right along beside you. Up front all the way."

"I'm engaged."

"Still?"

She made a strangled sound of wrath and started down the rubble-strewn hill. Zan came lazily after her. "Will you still be engaged, I wonder, after that post-luncheon conference? That should be a fascinating debate. Do you have negotiable items and rock-bottom basics?"

"On top of spying, you eavesdrop," she said bitterly. "I've never in all my life known anyone so shameless."

"In a good cause." His changeable eyes danced. "Besides, you haven't lived such a *long* life."

"A person like you makes it seem longer."

He wrinkled his brow. "I should have thought a life with Brandy would seem very long indeed. Is it a growing suspicion of that or shock at his unsuspected passion for trophies that's led to the afternoon summit meeting?"

"You have incredible gall! I wouldn't dream of discussing private matters with you."

"It might be better if you did."

"I can't see how."

He blocked her way. She stepped back, very conscious of the slow trembling that began in her when she came too near him, when his eyes caressed and searched her as they did now. "Do you need money, Tory? Is it important to you or is there some nonvisible reason why you have to have a lot?"

His tone was passionless, nonaccusing, but his daring to ask the question touched off her explosively contradictory feelings. "Of course I need money. Of course it's important to me. I have to pay my bills."

"What kind of bills?"

She caught in a furious breath and spaced her words. "That's none of your business. I don't know what your little game is, Zan Ericson, but I'm tired of being bullied and harassed and—"

She tried to dodge past him. A loose rock rolled from under her foot. She stumbled, snatched at air, and would have fallen if Zan hadn't caught her.

For a long moment she felt the strength of his arms, the deep steady beat of his heart. She stared up at him, bewildered at his fierce expression. "Tory," he said. "Tory. If you're in trouble—if you need something, please tell me. Don't do something you might regret."

Like fall in love with you? "I don't know what you're talking about," she muttered.

His face changed as if a smooth mask had fitted over it. He seemed to withdraw from her even before he firmly helped her get her footing and took his arms away.

"We'd better be getting down," he said.

Down by the canal a young girl was selling oranges that she peeled for the purchaser. Zan bought two and handed one to Tory. "It'll quench thirst better than Coke."

It did. As the juice trickled deliciously down her dry throat, Tory cast a side-glance at Zan, whose face still wore that dogged closed look.

What was he vexed about? She was the one with a right to be angry. Yet she couldn't whole-heartedly be except for occasional moments of head-on confrontation. Why was he sounding her out on money?

The disparaging implication was that she was marrying Brandy because he was well-to-do, but there could be another motive behind Zan's queries. He might be involved in some quick-money scheme—smuggling, drugs, gun-running. Maybe she seemed a potentially valuable Stateside contact. Or there might be some immediate way to use her. Don Luis could be part of the thing; it might be why he'd been so extraordinarily nice. Looking for an accomplice.

Shaky footing, trickier than that on the side of an overgrown ruin. Tory supposed that if she were totally committed to law and order she'd have pretended to take Zan's bait, play along till she knew what was going on.

With an intensity that shocked her, she knew she didn't want Zan to be doing anything wrong. "Zan," she said slowly, "do you need cash? Are you in trouble?"

Turning sharply, he stared at her with narrowed eyes that shone green. "Do you have a proposition?"

"Well, not right offhand." Her mind flew to her father's legacy. It wasn't a lot, but if Zan weren't too deeply mired, it might keep him from some desperate scheme. "I could loan you some money if that would help."

He gave a brittle laugh. "Not as much as I need, I'll bet. What can you spare?"

"Fifty thousand."

Zan whistled. "And I thought you and your aunt wrested only genteel poverty out of that bookshop."

"Aunt Elspeth never touched what my parents left," Tory said briefly.

They were nearing Dina's purple, pink, and gold resplendence. "Let's discuss it later," Zan said as Morgan came toward them. "And you'd better see how your fiancé feels about it."

Tory's heart sank at the thought. Brandy would never understand why she'd make such a loan to an almost stranger.

"It's my money and my business," she said.

"Oh? Well, I still think you'd better have your heart-to-heart first."

Morgan dragged him off to look at an emerald toucanet while Theron rounded up laggards and Narciso ceremoniously handed Tory up the steps.

"Woof-woof!" He chuckled softly to Mrs. Cunningham's offended stare. Tory laughed, but she was troubled as she sat down by her aunt.

It seemed horridly possible that Zan was in a tangle, one so bad that there was no retreat. Funny that he offered, with apparent sincerity, to help her when he seemed to be the one in need.

Whatever he'd done, she didn't believe that he was evil or that he'd hurt people. But if he got more and more involved in some shady or illegal undertaking, he might get trapped into doing things he'd never intended.

"Tory," said Elspeth anxiously, "don't you feel well?"

"Headache," Tory said.

Several of them. It was going to be a trying afternoon.

~ XIII ~

Tory blessed the fact that conversation wasn't needed at lunch, even though she was sitting next to Brandy. Beata and Mark Summerville were comparing Greek and Roman sculpture to that of the Mayas, pointing out that in both cases what was now classic white had once been flambuoyantly painted.

"I talked to one of the archaeologists in the museum," Beata said. "She told me the early red used at Palenque was a deep color, then the shade grew red-orange, and at the time of the collapse it had gone back to the first deep color."

"Some of the figures look almost Minoan with those concave bellies," Mark said. "And the work sculptors did! First they made the body, even to creating a perfect ankle that would later be covered by a boot. If they were doing a man, he'd first get a skirt, then the cummerbund, belt, and loincloth, with the belt looped through a buckle. Beads of stucco held on the various layers. It was quite a chore."

"And every time a relief needed new paint, they

put on a fresh layer of ground lime stucco and colored that," said Beata, marveling.

Dr. Cunningham smoothed his white mustache and came forth with the first statement Tory had ever heard him make. "The sculptures show that the royal line was afflicted with acromegaly. That is to say," he benignly explained, "that at least Lady Zac-Kuk had an overactive pituitary gland. She's portrayed with puffy eyes, swollen tongue, and an open mouth."

"Maybe she had a hangover," suggested Hal Callahan.

Dismissing that joke with a bleak smile, Dr. Cunningham pursued his subject. "Pacal's son, Chan-Bahlum, was polydactyl, so probably this, too, was a recurring characteristic in the family."

"Poly-what?" Mildred Halliday frowned.

"He had six toes and six fingers."

"My dear," rebuked Mrs. Cunningham faintly, "I wish you wouldn't. Not at lunch."

"What's wrong with six fingers?" the doctor demanded, snorting through his mustache. "Time's been when I wish I had eight or nine."

"Dearest."

Dearest subsided, grumbling, and Tory decided it was rather a good thing the Cunninghams kept to themselves. Hal and Beata began to talk about the chemical makeup of limestone and what had been used to keep the stucco moist.

Brandy turned to Tory with a smile. "Well, darling? My bungalow has a shady porch."

The sooner the better, Tory thought, though

her stomach shriveled into a knot and the headache that had been threatening declared itself
with electrical throbbing. Her state wasn't im-
proved by Zan's frowning gaze, which fixed on
her as she excused herself and rose.

Preceding Brandy, she felt as if the whole group
were watching them. "Relax, my love," he urged,
taking her arm. "You're all tensed up to give me a
lecture, but there's no reason why we can't be
comfortable while you're doing it. We'll have a
margarita, you can state your positions, I'll offer
mine, and we'll see what's to be done."

This was so far from the haughty declarations
of independence she had expected that Tory
glanced up in amazement and tripped at a dip in
the road. Brandy's hand steadied her and his smile
was winning as he gave a rueful shake of his head.

"Table conversation certainly has changed since
we started this tour," he remarked. "Acromegaly
and calcium carbonate!"

"I think it's good that people are less shy about
sharing what they know," Tory said.

"And you think it's time I did the same." Brandy
laughed. He tested a cane chair and placed it in
the shadiest part of the vine-covered porch front-
ing the small frame cabin. "All right, my love, I'll
fetch our margaritas and we'll play Truth or Consequences as long as you like, though I hope you'll
first allow me an opening statement that might
save you a lot of muddle."

Astonished and relieved at his manner, though
still wary, Tory sat down and reviewed the issues

so that she wouldn't be flimflammed into forgetting anything. But Brandy, handing her a salt-frosted margarita, toasted her with his own, and spoke before she could.

"The hunt's off, Victoria, at least for jaguars. I called on Don Luis this morning and we're still going into the wilds but just to see an especially beautiful shrine. A two-day trip: go tomorrow, spend the night, and return. Won't you come?"

Tory stared. "You—you're not going hunting?"

"No."

"But your guns, your hunting license . . ."

Brandy gave an elegant shrug and sipped his drink, regarding her with eyes that seemed to have no color of their own, mirroring the outside. "Let's put it in a nutshell, sweetheart. If I still meant to hunt, wouldn't you just about now be in the process of breaking our engagement?"

Cold fingers touched her heart, but she managed to sound calm. "It wasn't just the hunting, Brandy, though I'd never have guessed you went in for it. That's something we'll have to talk about, because I can't stand the thought of killing wild things for pleasure." She looked straight at him and tried not to let her voice waver. "Why didn't you mention the hunting license? It was so much trouble to get that you can't just have forgotten it."

He set down his glass, placed hers beside it, and took her hands, carrying them to either side of his lean face. "No doubt it was subterranean and reprehensible, darling, but make some allowance for the fact that at my age a man doesn't have unnecessary showdowns. It seemed likely that a chance to do any really interesting hunting wouldn't come up on this trip, but Yucatán's renowned for its game and I couldn't resist being ready."

"Figuring you could deal with my objections when they came up."

"*If* they did." Slowly, caressingly, Brandy kissed her palms. "We'd never talked about it, but I have to admit that I suspected, after our marriage, that my rare hunts would be rarer yet."

"I don't know what to say. I detest married people trying to limit or force each other. But hunting—" Tory hunched her shoulders. "I hate it, Brandy."

He raised his head, gazed at her with eyes like molten steel. "You *would* break our engagement, wouldn't you?"

She thought, pictured him coming home with a deer or jaguar. "I wouldn't marry a hunter. I couldn't!"

His mouth tightened before he sat up, releasing her. "Don't get wound up, Victoria. As I said I hunt only for unusual trophies. It's not that important to me."

Tory felt guilty, as if she'd used blackmail and childish displays to win her point while Brandy was adult and magnanimous. But, darn him, he was the one who'd tacitly deceived her, avoided a subject on which he'd suspected they'd clash. He seemed to guess her feelings, said with amused tenderness, "Cheated you out of a noble stand, haven't I? But, my very dear, with advancing age comes a sense of priorities. I don't have to prove I'm a man by battling you over something that matters to you infinitely more than it can to me." For a tolerant moment he watched her struggle with this before he gave his burnished head a coaxing tilt. "Now then, you've carried the field. Won't you be generous and visit the shrine?"

Why not? She'd still have several days to see Palenque and a trip into the rain forests would be something special. She could scarcely refuse to please Brandy when he had, without argument, given up the hunt he'd gone to enormous trouble to be ready for.

"Don Luis says I can go?"

"He's absolutely enchanted at the thought."

Tory gave a little nod. "All right. I'd better tell Elspeth and get my gear packed."

Brandy rose along with her. "Thanks, love," he said softly. "It'll be wonderful to have you to myself, away from all these people."

"There'll be Don Luis and the guides."

"Yes. But, thank God, no Alexander Ericson!"

For a moment, in her sense of renewed closeness with Brandy, she almost told him of her worries about Zan, her fear he might be breaking the law. But Brandy didn't like Zan and probably wouldn't try to help him. If there was a chance, she'd sound Don Luis on the matter. He was Zan's partner, seemed fond of him.

A sudden unwelcome thought struck her like a

chill wind. What if Don Luis were Zan's partner in more than the swim shop? He had openly admitted that he was on the watch for ways to get more money, rich as he apparently was. If Zan was in trouble it was entirely possible that Don Luis had put him there.

"Why the frown?" Brandy smoothed between her eyebrows with the heel of his thumb, turned up her face, and kissed her long and lingeringly. Tory found herself responding, but not in the same total way she had used to. She must have been too worried about Zan. Brandy seemed aware of her constraint, for he shifted his lips to her throat.

"I want you to myself again," he whispered against her cheek. "I had no idea that this tour would provide us with two dozen chaperones."

No use in pointing out to him that group tours weren't designed for intimacy, except with one's roommate. Tory murmured something and said she'd see him at dinner.

Elspeth shared her surprise that Brandy would forgo his custom-tailored jaguar hunt, but thought his willingness to drop trophy-collecting indicated maturity and the value he placed on his relationship with Tory.

"A man who likes you less because you have your own ideas isn't worth having." She sighed. "At least that's what I tell myself about Theron."

Tory had to laugh. "Elspeth, an ornithologist

can't appreciate having identification constantly
disputed!"

"I did quit that when you made me see what
I was doing," said Elspeth mournfully.

"But by then you had him scared to death."
Tory gave her aunt a comforting hug. "Never
mind! Invite him to see your rare-bird book collection on his way back north. Let him pore over
your first edition John James Audubon while you
ply him with Southern rum cream cake."

Elspeth's hazel eyes lit up. "Tory, that's a
great idea! I think corn fritters and cheese grits
would be more his thing, but I do have those
lovely old books and portfolios."

"So invite him!" Tory laughed.

"I just will," decided Elspeth. "I'd rather be
turned down than go around kicking myself for
not trying to get the first man I've really liked
since your uncle passed on." She swung her feet
up on the bed out of Tory's way. "You'll be gone
only overnight?"

"That's what Brandy says." Tory emptied the
small nylon duffel she'd brought to hold shoes and
laundry. "A change of clothes and a toothbrush is
about all I'll need, but you'll at least have a little
more room to move around in."

It didn't take long to pack; Tory even managed
to put her feet up and rest ten minutes before the
four-o'clock birdwalk.

After an almost birdless expedition to a field
along the river, it was a rather tired group that

assembled for dinner, but by the time people got to *flan* and coffee and Don Luis appeared, energies were rising and everyone, including Narciso, moved over to the largest thatched shelter for the party.

Hal had agreed to be master of ceremonies and took the center of the floor with a flourishing bow, looking quite boyish as he shook his tight gold curls.

"*Compañeros,*" he said, "tonight marks an epoch for bird-watchers. With your help and dedication that execrable use of a noun we hold in reverence, the use of 'bird' as a verb, can come to a halt. No longer will the retort: 'Oh, *bird* you!' rise to one's lips when invited to seek for immature whatnots and rose-breasted thrashers." He paused and extended his hand to Frieda. "Beloved, yours shall be the historic honor of bestowing this new verb upon the bird-loving world."

Frieda swept a curtsy and laughed up at him. "Thanks for your generosity, but you thought of it all by yourself." She faced the audience and spoke with solemn distinctness. "Orn. We orn, you orn, they orn. Orn, fellow bird-watchers, is the verb of the future."

"'A-orning we will go!" whooped Zan, and led the clapping, though there were enough quizzical glances to make it doubtful that Hal's pet aversion was going to drop from use.

Etheridge Martin startled everyone by singing some earthy songs from colonial times. Narciso had borrowed a guitar from one of the cooks and almost brought down the thatch with several stirring Spanish songs and a very old one in Maya. Then Mildred took the guitar and Tory went to stand by her, holding the notebook with their song.

"You can all join in on the choruses," Mildred said. "This song is dedicated to the barkless dogs of the ancient Mayas, so sing out for them, folks!"

Mildred had a strong sweet voice that Tory only needed to follow and after the first "Cu-cu-cu-cu-ruuu", everyone joined in, even the Bowdries and the Cunninghams. Everyone but Brandy. When the song ended, he had on the polite mask that Tory had learned often concealed anger. He rose, though, as did Don Luis, to let her sit between them.

"Charming," murmured Don Luis. "During our trip, you must teach me that song. It would amuse my children."

"Your children?" Tory stammered.

Don Luis' tawny eyes shone. "I have four very beautiful children."

"And a wife?" asked Tory, goaded.

"Of course." Don Luis shrugged, adding with a scapegrace smile that made Tory laugh in spite of her indignation, "She's married, but I'm not."

Mark Summerville did an astonishing number of bird songs on his clarinet and then played old dance numbers that soon had most of the group maneuvering about the small floor to "Stardust," "Smoke Gets in Your Eyes," and "Old Black Magic."

Brandy danced with Tory first. He was gracefully expert with a subtle but definite lead, and any annoyance he'd felt with her over the singing seemed to melt as he held her in his arms.

"It's going to be marvelous to get you away from this mob," he said. "It seems ages since we've really been alone—oh, damn! Here comes Don Luis!"

Don Luis kept a respectable distance, which was fortunate since even so he radiated an overwhelming masculinity that would have been formidable except for his good humor.

"I am overjoyed, *señorita*, that you're coming on the trip," he said. "We shall have a chance to become . . . acquainted."

Tory couldn't help laughing. "That's almost exactly what my fiancé just said."

Don Luis shook his head reprovingly. "Don Brandon seems a man of the world, but what could induce him to bring you on such a tour rather than a honeymoon—"

"He didn't bring me," Tory explained. "This was a gift from me to my aunt. Brandy decided to come, too. I'm afraid he's been sadly bored, but he didn't have to come."

Don Luis' eyes widened. "But of course he did!"

"I can't see why. He's completely indifferent to birds and seems to have brought his business right along." Tory nipped off what sounded perilously close to complaint. Don Luis knew how to bend a sympathetic ear, but in practice he must be more chauvinist than Brandy.

Swinging her about, Don Luis chuckled. "No

man of Don Brandon's cultivated tastes is going to risk having the lady who finally pleases him swept away by some stranger under the influence of a Caribbean moon. Not that he's managed to guard you entirely. Here comes that rascal Zan."

That was so like Brandy's frustrated comment on Don Luis' approach that Tory was laughing when Zan danced her away.

"Belle of the ball," he teased.

"Not much competition," she retorted. "But it's fun." Her last words wavered.

Zan didn't hold her especially close, but his touch sent a warm tingling awareness through her and his gaze seemed to plunge deep, touching her heart and mind.

"At least you can't say what Don Luis and Brandy did," she said, struggling to defuse the atmosphere. "They're looking forward to the trip." At Zan's puzzled look, she remembered. "Oh, you don't know! The jaguar hunt's off. Don Luis is taking Brandy to see a remote shrine instead. And I'm going."

Zan's arm tightened convulsively. They were near the edge of the shelter and he danced her right off the cement, drawing her into the trees that grew up close around the building.

"You're going into the back country?" he demanded. "Don Luis consented?"

Tory tried to escape, realized his fingers might as well have been steel clamps. "Don Luis seems delighted to have me. And it's just an overnight."

"I don't like it. You shouldn't go."

Stunned at this flat assertion, Tory gave an incredulous laugh. "I can't recall your being named my guardian."

"Well, you need one. I'm shocked at Don Luis. Back in the forests a lot of things can happen. In fact, if you got off a path right around here, you could be so lost in ten minutes that you might never be found."

"We'll have Lacandon guides and I don't intend to go wandering off."

"No one ever does."

His grim manner worried Tory in spite of herself, but she scoffed, trying again to draw her hands away. "Don Luis knows the country as well or better than you, surely. He wouldn't let me go if it were as dangerous as you say."

"Don Luis is not in love with you."

Tory gasped. Before she could move, Zan took her mouth with his, fiercely, achingly. His arms were hard and unrelenting as his lips. She fought, trying to wrench free, but he only drew her closer, kissed her till she had no strength, till she would have fallen if he hadn't held her, till at last her arms, independent of her conscious will, crept up and closed around his neck.

"I love you," he said harshly, lifting his head at last. "Tory, you must love me back, or I wouldn't feel this way!"

"I—I don't know!" Tory touched her mouth with her fingers, shakenly happy yet bewildered and worried. "You make all kinds of things happen for me, Zan, but I don't know—"

"I know about me," he said. "And I don't want my girl off in the jungle without me."

Tory stiffened. "Don't come, Zan. Please. I—I need time to think."

He gazed at her a long long time. "You will be careful?" He hesitated, spoke in a burst, "Tory, if—if you were in trouble, you'd tell me? You wouldn't do something crazy?"

"That," she couldn't help saying, "is exactly what I'd like to ask you. Are you in trouble, Zan? Do you need money?"

Abruptly, almost as if he were angry, he dropped her hand. "I guess we both need to think," he said.

At the edge of the cement, they began to dance again, but her heart was heavy now, and her feet seemed to drag. She was glad when Mark blew an alert.

"We're founding a new order tonight," he announced when the dancing stopped. "Each member is hereby declared a founding member of the Honorable Order of the Wild Goose Chase. For each outing you take to find a bird you don't locate, you get a feather, and our guest, Don Luis, has brought enough shed feathers to get you off to a good start. He's also brought bottles for the nightcaps you'd better have now before we break up."

There was laughter and toasting, but Zan's face was closed. Tory said a quick good night, told Don Luis she'd be ready in the morning, and was glad that Brandy, who saw her to her room, seemed no more disposed to talk than she and dropped the briefest of kisses on her cheek.

"Tomorrow," he said. "Be ready at five." But though he smiled, his silver eyes seemed cold and Tory was glad to escape inside.

She couldn't escape the weltering confusion of her thoughts and feelings, though.

What was the matter with her? Engaged to one man, responding to another as she had to Zan; not sure which she loved, or since she could be so bewildered, whether she loved either one, really. The way she felt about Zan was a storm, wild, encompassing, defying reason. She was afraid of that. Especially if his recklessness had led him into some serious tangle.

Yet when he'd kissed her, nothing else had mattered. She'd only wanted to stay in his arms. Tossing restlessly, she knew it was a good thing she was going off tomorrow, away from Zan—where she could think.

~⊰ XIV ⊱~

It was just lightening a bit from full darkness when the jeep pulled up in front and Tory tiptoed out without waking her aunt. Don Luis, in the driver's seat, handed back a thermos of coffee, and Brandy, who'd jumped out of the back to help Tory in, offered a napkin-wrapped basket of *pan dulce*. Don Luis gave her an appreciative good morning and presented the swarthy man beside him.

"This is Florentino, *señorita*. He knows this country better than anybody and we are much obliged to him for guiding when there will not be hunting of jaguars. He has no English and little Spanish."

Florentino inclined his head while Tory said, "*Mucho gusto*." A smile flickered across the Indian's pockmarked face. He had long black hair, but he wore jeans and a cotton plaid shirt.

"We'll drive as far as we can," said Don Luis, putting the jeep in gear. "Then Florentino's cousins will take us down the river by raft till we need to strike through the forest. It won't be monotonous."

"The shrine sounds a little like the Cave of Balankanche," Brandy said, voice taut with excitement. "There's a cavern leading into the side of a hill downward to a lake. The stalactites and stalagmites are quite fantastic, but there's a jade jaguar that must be worth a fortune and many smaller figures."

"You will be the first and probably the last living *norteamericanos* to see the shrine," said Don Luis, expertly taking the jeep over a jolting rutted way that had turned off the main road. "The Lacandones consider it very holy. Florentino had to get permission from the headman of the nearest village. If this visit brought a lot of people rushing to the shrine, Florentino's health would suffer.

Don Luis asked Florentino a few questions in his language, nodded at the answers, and called back over his shoulder. "Last year a guide brought an archaeologist who tried to take pictures. Both men vanished. Florentino thinks they're at the bottom of the lake."

Tory's scalp prickled. "I didn't know the shrine was *that* holy," she murmured.

"What would be the use of a trip like this if it weren't?" Brandy questioned, one eyebrow arching. He patted a holster that Tory hadn't, in the semi-night, noticed till now. "Don't fret, love. We're armed and I must say I haven't been much impressed by the Lacandon arrows I've seen."

"Tipped with a little frog venom they can kill a man," warned Don Luis. "And you must have some idea of what machetes can do."

"The question won't arise," said Brandy with a confidence Tory was far from feeling. He squeezed her hand and smiled. "Don't worry, sweetheart. The thing to remember is that we're being privileged to see something almost no one from our world can."

"I suppose so." Tory couldn't feel wildly enthusiastic. It certainly was more of an experience to view ruins and shrines in comparative solitude without the jostle of crowds, but she couldn't imagine valuing a beautiful thing less because others could see it. Her impulse, when she found something good or interesting or lovely, was to share it with people she thought would appreciate it. "I'm glad the Lacandones have their private place, but I'm not sure that we should see it."

At Brandy's frown, she shrugged defiantly. "I mean, I don't care anything about being the only *gringa* to see the shrine."

Don Luis chuckled. "What a—*democratic* attitude," he teased.

"One I don't have," said Brandy tightly. "I place absolutely no value on what others can share."

Hunching his shoulders in mock alarm, Don Luis brought them skillfully over a series of teeth-rattling bumps before he grinned back at Tory. "My opinion of you soars even higher, *señorita*. You must be unique to attract such a connoisseur."

Brandy was not one to display his feelings. Tory stared in surprise when he said, "Victoria is the first woman I've wished to marry."

"I can understand that," said Don Luis with roguish gallantry. "If I weren't married, I'd want to marry her, too."

"How fortunate," said Brandy, "that you are married."

Uncomfortable at being discussed like some art object, Tory was glad that the road, if it could still be called that, got so bad that it demanded all of Don Luis' attention and the jolting made conversation impractical.

The jungle pressed in on either side and from the top, where vines and limbs sometimes barely cleared their heads. There were orchids and air plants and the flash of parrots and toucans. The naked red bark of the gumbo-limbo stood out against luxuriant foliage and an occasional white-barked tree. The brilliant yellow flowers of the wild cotton tree looked like poppies blooming in a field of leaves. There were pink and white kapok blooms and the air was so thick with scent and moisture that it was intoxicating, like a weight in the body.

They lurched into a grassy plain that stretched to a river that resembled a huge lazily undulating serpent coiling through the high grass and trees. Several turkeys fled from their way, and Tory recognized them as the ocellated kind from their blue heads dotted with red warts. Hosts of waterfowl rose at the jeep's roaring approach. Tory gasped in wonder, able only to recognize them as herons, egrets, and several kinds of ducks.

Don Luis nodded at a stand of trees in the high

grass. "Bet there's more turkey in those trees and at least half-a-dozen deer. These grassy savannas are good places to hunt, though game won't flush till you're almost on top of it. Jungle hunting has to be done mostly at night with lights, mating calls, live animals staked out for bait—oh, forgive me, *señorita*. I forgot your prejudice." Don Luis touched Florentino's shoulder in a congratulatory way. "Florentino can tell in the dark what an animal is just from its eyes. And there are his cousins. Good. I hoped they wouldn't keep us waiting. Time doesn't mean much to forest Lacandones."

Brandy laughed. "Perhaps money does."

"Not as much as one might think," Don Luis said. "As long as the big lumbering concerns leave them some uncleared jungle, most Lacandones prefer to live as they have for centuries."

"They can't have long," Brandy said. "With hardwoods getting scarcer, all this great mahogany won't be left just to shelter a few remnant savages."

Don Luis swung the jeep into a stand of trees. "Maybe. But for a few years I wouldn't undertake to quarrel with a Lacandon in his forests."

Florentino introduced his kinsmen as they came up and began unloading gear. Cruz was knobbily skinny with a sweet, childlike smile that contrasted with a puckered scar running from cheekbone to chin. Enrique was broad and short with white strong teeth and a broken nose. He was supposed to stay with the jeep, and after he had helped stow the baggage on the raft, where it was lashed securely in the middle, he went back to the vehicle.

Tory perched on some supply boxes while Brandy and Don Luis sat on packs of other equipment. "There's a guest hut in the village," said Don Luis. "We can sling our hammocks there and use plenty of insect repellent."

Something along the riverbank that looked like a muddy log suddenly moved, settling into the water. Tory gasped and pointed. Don Luis grinned. "Crocodiles aren't very dangerous, *señorita*. Just don't tempt them."

"I won't if I can help it," Tory said fervently.

By the time she'd seen a few more of the fantastically well-camouflaged creatures, she was able to accept them as part of the scene, though, as with rattsnakes, she had no wish for close acquaintance. As Florentino and Cruz poled along, water birds rose from their course. Don Luis pointed out a spider monkey whose noisy progress through the trees was far more audible than visible.

"These river areas are full of game," he said. "Deer and peccary, of course, armadillo, puma, agouti, kinkajou, ring-tailed cat, fox, coatimundi, raccoon, and hosts of birds like the crested guan and tinamou. But they're all extremely cautious; you could look all day without seeing one." He considered for a moment. "It would be interesting to know what Señor Bowdrie would sense in an area like this."

"Why Bowdrie in particular?" Brandy voiced the question Tory had in mind.

Don Luis looked at them in surprise. "You didn't know he's almost blind?"

"Oh, no," cried Tory.

"I'm afraid so," Don Luis assured her gently. "This is the last bird trip they'll probably go on. But I talked with them a good bit at the party last night. He relies now more on bird songs, of course, but he said that he is entering a new world—increased sensitivity to touch, atmosphere, and equilibrium, all the more subtle ways of knowing that sight tends to overwhelm."

So that was why the Bowdries had seemed withdrawn, why they seemed to prefer each other's company. "He has always wished to see the birds of Yucatán," Don Luis went on. "He says he is storing their images so that just as one might look at slides or photos, he can call them up and 'see' with his memory."

Tory was glad that Don Luis had dimensions beyond getting richer and playboying, but she felt ashamed that a stranger had taken the trouble to know some of her traveling companions better than she did. At noon they stopped at a rocky sandbar and had lunch—shredded turkey, avocado, and onion wrapped in soft *tostadas,* cheese stuffed with meat and eggs, bananas, more nutcrusted *pan dulce,* and thermoses of iced coffee.

It was hot and the humidity intensified it. Tory's skin felt plugged with first sunscreen and then moisture, and her trousers and shirt clung soggily to her. The guides rigged a tarpaulin shade, and everyone rested for an hour before clambering back on the raft.

It was mid-afternoon when Florentino poled

for an alligator-shaped rock promontory jutting out in the water. Banking the raft, he and Cruz held the craft steady while the passengers got off and then unloaded the duffels and supplies. There was stirring in the heavy growth, and a burro emerged, batting his ears at insects, his long protruding teeth as stained as if he'd been chewing tobacco.

He was followed by a slender young man with beautiful dark eyes and smooth skin. Florentino introduced him as Pablo, another cousin. He seemed absolutely fascinated with Tory, and though he helped load the little gray beast, every time Tory looked his direction, he was staring at her.

"Last part of the journey," Don Luis encouraged. "We should be in the village in an hour and have time to visit the cavern before night." He seemed to guess Tory's reaction, for his topaz eyes were sympathetic though he laughed. "And that's not all, *señorita*. The headman, Don Carlos, will want to entertain us tonight. His father was Spanish and saw that Carlos was educated, though Carlos as a young man returned to his mother's people. This will be your chance to see if you like *balché*. That's native beer."

Tory couldn't stifle a dismayed sound. Don Luis chuckled consolingly. "The party may be a good thing, *compañera*. Since you aren't used to hammocks, the night may seem very long to you even if we're up late."

Cruz led the way along a fairly wide path. The

burro followed, escorted by the lithe Pablo; Tory walked behind Brandy and in front of Don Luis; and Florentino brought up the rear. He said something to Don Luis, who made an appreciative exclamation and translated the news.

"Someone brought in a *tepescuintle* today. That's a small piglike creature that furnishes the best meal you could have when it's seasoned with herbs and steamed in banana leaves in a pit lined with red-hot rocks."

"But we can't eat a lot of their food, can we?" asked Tory.

"We'd better or they'll be offended. But don't worry about it," Don Luis advised. "I've brought coffee, chocolate, nuts, dates, rice, beans, and lots of condensed milk, which Carlos loves. You needn't worry, *señorita,* about eating the food that teems in the forest."

It was good to walk after hours on the raft, but Tory felt as if she were suffocating, breathing in liquid rather than air. Gradually, she found there *was* enough oxygen to keep her going, and when she relaxed, the heavy, oppressive sensation lessened so that she could thrill to brilliant flowers and the majesty of the great trees with their drapings of vines. It was odd not to hear Theron call, "Collared trogon at four o'clock," and not to have her binoculars weighting her neck, but she did see trogons anyway, and both green and Aztec parakeets as well as several kinds of hummingbirds and some spectacular toucans.

One moment they were in the jungle. The next

they emerged abruptly in a clearing. Several dozen thatched huts and open-sided roofed shelters were scattered about. Children of all ages came to watch the strangers and stared especially at Tory before they melted back to make room for a sturdy keen-faced man of middle years who came forward to exchange an *abrazo* with Don Luis. After they were through patting each other on the shoulder, Don Luis made introductions and Don Carlos greeted them in Spanish, which Don Luis translated.

He and his people were glad, Don Carlos said, to show Don Luis' friends a very holy thing, for Don Luis would not bring anyone here who would not properly revere the shrine. Don Carlos would not keep them now, since it was getting late, but he looked forward to their company that evening.

Don Luis returned courtesies while Florentino saw their belongings were unloaded at a hut slightly larger than the rest that stood in the center of the village. Two young pretty women in white cotton shifts brought gourds of a fermented brew that Tory could only manage a few sips of, though Brandy got through his and Don Luis tossed his off and reached for hers, laughing and saying something to Don Carlos, who looked curiously at Tory but smiled as he answered.

"I told him *balché* is too strong a drink for young *norteamericanas*," Don Luis explained. "And he said he is glad to know this for all the *norteamericanas* he used to know could drink a *chiclero* under the table—that's like saying they outdrank the lumberjacks."

"Mmm," said Tory. Then she saw the twitching at the edge of Don Carlos' lips and couldn't keep from bursting into laughter. He laughed, too. Don Luis exploded. Florentino, Cruz, and Pablo caught the infection. For several minutes everyone laughed. Except for Brandy, who had walked to the edge of the village and waited with an impatient set to his lean tall body.

Impulsively, Tory offered her hand to Don Carlos. He shook it and bowed, but laughter still danced deep in his eyes as they exchanged farewells. Only Florentino went with the visitors, leading them up a narrow trail that quickly left the village as obscured from view as if it had been miles away. The path was not much used and Florentino frequently had to clear the way with his machete as it wound along the side of a hill to where a fall of stones stretched on either side of a hole leading into blackness, so shrouded with vines that it was hard to see.

Florentino led the way in, turning on his flashlight. Don Luis signaled Tory and Brandy to follow while he brought up the rear with another flash. They could stand up, but the passage was narrow and the hard earth underneath was slippery. Something brushed Tory's cheek and she choked back a scream. She knew that rabid bats were much more likely to be comatose and avoid people than to attack them, but they were still not her favorite mammal.

Nor, she had to admit, were caves her favorite places. They seemed to be just waiting for the lights to go out so they could swallow you alive. The dank air was full of odors of earth and decay. This must be how a grave would smell. . . .

Stop it, she told herself. Four strong men and two flashlights! How silly can you get?

But the air grew thicker and perspiration beaded her face and soaked her shirt between her shoulder blades. She felt dizzy, almost nauseated, and was on the point of saying she had to stop for a moment when Florentino climbed into a crawl way.

Gritting her teeth, Tory followed him, hoping that she wouldn't put her hands down on some reptile. The sooner they saw the shrine and got out the happier she'd be, but it would have been ridiculous to back out now.

Florentino's light played wildly as he came out of the tunnel. He shone the beam on a chiseled wonderland of whitish stalagmites and stalactites filling the large chamber. Tory caught in her breath at the wonderful giant iciclelike masses, stained different colors by minerals and time. Then the lights moved to touch gleaming greenish water. A thronelike altar was carved in the side of the stone; on this stretched a most beautiful jaguar of jade so dark it looked almost black. It was a little over a foot long.

A miracle it had escaped looters. Tory turned from gazing at it to be startled at the glow in Brandy's eyes.

"Magnificent!" he breathed. His hands curved as if touching it, feeling the polished shape. "Utterly magnificent."

Tory was irrationally glad when Don Luis said it was time to go.

~XV~

The pretty young woman who had brought them *balché* showed Tory a spring in shouting distance of the village where she could wash. This done, she changed into clean clothes in the guest hut, combed her hair, and came out feeling considerably fresher.

A delicious tangy odor filled the air as the *tepescuintle* was brought out of the pit and unwrapped from the layers of banana leaves where it was left for carving. There were pots of corn soup and plump tamales, gourds of *balché*. Sitting on mats in the large central thatched shelter, the men of the village entertained the visitors while the women and children peered out of huts or watched and whispered at a distance.

The tasty porklike steamed meat and tamales could be eaten with fingers, but Tory only pretended to dip from the bowl of gruel she shared with five other people. She also merely pretended to drink from the *balché* when it was passed to her several times; when she did this, she caught Don Carlos' amused glance.

Don Luis, of course, had to speak for the strangers, and though he translated back to Tory and Brandy, she suspected that he censored some of the remarks at which he burst into hearty laughter. She was also a bit shy about being the only woman at the feast, and was glad when at last Don Carlos stood up and she could politely stretch her cramped legs and body.

"*Buenas noches, señorita,*" said Don Carlos, bowing. He added something, and Don Luis folded him in another *abrazo* before he turned to explain. "When one of them is going on a dangerous journey, the Lacandones sometimes appeal for a safe trip by burning incense in the god pots and offering *balché* and food. Don Carlos will make this chant for us tonight so that we may travel protected tomorrow. It is a great honor."

"Tell him he's very kind," said Brandy in a bored voice, but Tory went over and once again shook the headman's hand.

"*Mil gracias,* Don Carlos."

He smiled at her and moved away.

"Better tuck in," said Don Luis. "We'll make an early start tomorrow. Señorita, your hammock is slung. Shall I show you how to get in?"

"Please."

In the almost dark hut, he planted his derriere firmly in the middle of the net and swung up his feet in one easy motion. "If you try to climb in, it'll dump you," he said. "But have a good base and you'll do fine. Hammocks are an excellent idea. They do away with bedding and they're much cooler than beds."

"I suppose so," said Tory without much enthusiasm. She was sure her neck would be permanently ensconced in her shoulder by morning, but was too tired to care, too tired to really mind that she would be sleeping in her clothes. It would be heaven just to stretch out and close her eyes.

Brandy's hammock was hung under the thatched roof built onto the hut, and Don Luis had found his own situation. After he'd said good night and disappeared into the shadows, Brandy stepped into the hut, stood outlined in the door.

"Good night, my love." He kissed her lightly, more fleetingly than he ever had, and though it wasn't the time or place for a passionate embrace, Tory was puzzled.

She slipped off her shoes, socks, and belt, loosened her clothing, and hoisted herself carefully into the hammock. She couldn't seem to fit her shoulder, arm, and head comfortably. Her last clear thought was that she'd never go to sleep. And then she was.

She woke sharp and clear as if there'd been a sound, but she heard nothing now, though she strained and held her breath, staying motionless in spite of the twist of her neck. It must have been late, for there was moonlight beyond the hut. The village seemed absolutely hushed, yet she felt as if there had been something . . . some warning. . . .

Stealthily lifting her head, she peered about. There was no one in the hut. She eased her feet out of the hammock, stood up, and though nervous of spiders and reptiles, moved barefoot to the door and looked out.

Brandy's hammock was empty. But up the side of the mountain bulking eerily in the light of the shrunken moon blinked a light.

Then it vanished. Tory stood feeling quite sick and bewildered, a dreadful suspicion forming, though she tried to shake it off, think of other explanations.

It didn't have to be Brandy at the cave. He might have just gone for a stroll because he found the hammock hard to sleep in. But she couldn't help remembering: Brandy's remarks about the treasures of Balankanche being wasted, his collector's instinct and need to possess rarities, his excitement over the jaguar.

She was afraid, much afraid, that he had gone to the cave to steal the priceless jade image. For a moment she thought of trying to find Don Luis and asking for his help, but she hated to accuse Brandy if she wasn't positive. Besides, maybe she could convince him that he shouldn't take the jaguar and no one would have to know.

As she went back to her shoes, shook out them as well as her socks before pulling them on, another frightening possibility flashed through her mind. What if Don Luis and Brandy were partners in art theft? Such an alliance could be lucrative for them both. She remembered the mysterious trip to Cancún, Brandy's astonishing amount of business, his total lack of interest in the tour.

And Zan?

Her heart turned painfully at the thought and her feelings cried against it, but the chance couldn't be discounted. He *was* Don Luis' partner. With or without him, he could easily be an art smuggler on at least a casual basis. She hated to even dream of such a thing, but it could be true.

She didn't relish making her way through the forests at night. The jade jaguar might have muscle-and-bone relatives prowling about and there were undoubtedly snakes and probably dangerous creatures she didn't know about. She wouldn't dare use a light, and the idea of going back into that cavern in the complete darkness made her stomach turn to a heavy tight mass of knots. She looked around for some kind of weapon, but found none, decided to lose no more time, and slipped through the village toward the path that led up the mountain. After a bit of search, she found it.

Ghostly light spangled the jungle floor, made the leaves shine with mystical brilliance muting into shadows. Something moved now and then in the dense undergrowth, and a bird screamed. In the distance came a stifled whimper and a slight sound of impact. Tory shivered. Some little thing had fallen prey to a larger. It was the round of natural life, but she didn't like it. The night jungle was menacing and full of unknown threats.

She wished Zan were with her. She wouldn't be afraid then. The unbidden wish came before she could repulse it, making her in this deep night, alone with her fears and naked feelings, admit what she had refused till now to confront.

She loved Zan. Zan, not Brandy. And she'd love him even if he were mixed up in something crooked; she couldn't help it, though that didn't change the wrongs of the matter if he were doing wrong. And she didn't know how he felt about her. To him she was probably just another *norte-americana* of whom there were many more coming.

However all that was, she would still try to keep Brandy from taking the jaguar if that was indeed his intent. But she'd have to tell him, soon, that their engagement was a mistake. For some reason, he'd thought she was unusual enough to collect as his wife, but she could never fit that role. For her part, she had been dazzled and flattered at being valued and wooed by such an experienced, worldly, and attractive man.

They had both been victims of their own illusions. She'd enjoyed his making her feel beautiful, rare, and entrancing. She hadn't liked it a bit when he scolded her as a teacher might upbraid a slow student. He had a lot to communicate to some suitable, receptive woman, but Tory knew she could never exist in the invisible showcase cage he'd keep her in.

That was over. And in spite of her present terrible fear and aloneness, a kind of pressure lifted from her. She seemed to breathe more deeply than she had in months. It was as if some sealed-off portion of her came to life again; at any other moment she would have wanted to sing.

The cave entrance loomed before her now. As she looked in, a vagrant gold haze seemed to come from the tunnel ahead, perhaps reflected from the light she'd seen before. That was a little better than absolute pitch blackness, apart from the necessity to move without sound. Wouldn't do to go blundering into walls. She hoped she wouldn't meet a flock of bats, but she braced herself for that or any sudden fright.

If the light wasn't Brandy's or if it proved that he'd just come to look again at the supremely handsome sculpture, she'd rather he didn't know she'd followed.

Taking a deep breath, she started into the depths. She remembered that the roof was highest in the center and held her arms above her head slightly to act as antennae if she started to waver into a head-bumping course.

Her fingers brushed rock now and then, sometimes dry, sometimes wet, always cold. Once she brushed what felt like soft fur and swallowed a scream.

Here was the crawl through. Glad that at least she'd been through the cavern and knew there were no drop-offs or large side exits that she was likely to blunder down.

At the end of the tunnel, she saw soft light and

was both grateful and afraid. Light was wonderfully welcome after the darkness, but if she could see, so could the light's owner. She hoped desperately that she'd be able to learn all that was important from the tunnel, not have to creep out through the masses of stalagmites.

She didn't know what she'd do if the explorer weren't Brandy, so she concentrated on hoping that she'd find him admiring the jaguar and ready to start back with just the memory. If he reached for the actual object . . .

She'd have to come out of hiding and urge him to leave it alone, threaten to tell the Lacandones if he wouldn't respect their holy place. He'd be furious, but there wouldn't be much he could do but yield.

Inching along on her knees, Tory's back ached and her hands tingled with the expectation of touching something slimy or squirmy, but there only moist hard earth embedded with occasional was only moist hard earth embedded with occasional stones. The light grew brighter as she neared the end of the narrow passage and she moved more slowly, pausing to crane her neck forward and see as far as she could.

The chamber glowed faint gold, and now she saw the glittering mineral growths etching fantastic shapes among the shadows. She was only a few feet from the great room when the underground river shimmered into view and with it a sight that ended any hope or uncertainty.

Brandy was stepping from the water with the

jaguar in his hands. The flashlight beamed from a ledge, and he stooped by it to wrap the jade figure in one of his jackets. A length of rope lay beside the flash. Apparently he meant to lash the booty to him so that he could get through the crawl way more easily.

Even though this was what she'd feared, Tory's heart plunged sickeningly. Why? Why couldn't he love beautiful things without needing to have them?

She must have made some inadvertent sound, for his silver-gold head lifted and he reached for the pistol at his belt. "Who is it? Who's there?"

"It's me." Tory scrambled out, ran forward. "Oh, Brandy! Don't do this! The people have been so kind to us and they don't have much."

"No reason why a pack of ignorant savages should hoard away such a treasure," he snapped, then said more calmly, silver eyes dwelling on hers hypnotically, "I have a museum buyer for this, Victoria. It'll be admired by hundreds of thousands of art lovers, not wasted down here in a jungle."

"And you'll make a small fortune."

He shrugged and smiled. "Well, my dear, most fiancées never complain of impending wealth."

"I—I wouldn't touch such money. You can't take the jaguar! I won't let you!"

The dark pupil swelled in his eyes, leaving only a thin pale gray rim. "Just how will you stop me, dearest?"

"Don't you care what I think?"

His mouth twisted. "Victoria, my lovely, if this little discovery shatters you, may I assure you that it's nothing compared to what I felt last night when I saw you in Ericson's arms? Don't try to pretend that you were fighting him."

"No. I wasn't."

Brandy shrugged lightly, but a ripple of tautly controlled anger ran through his voice. "Then let's not talk nonsense." He finished wrapping the jaguar, got to his feet.

"I'll tell Don Carlos," she said in a gasp. "I mean it, Brandy. I won't let you steal this!"

He gazed at her for a long moment and sighed "Well, that leaves me no choice, does it? I still desire you, Victoria, but you're useless to me as a mistress or wife because of that Caribbean Peter Pan. I want the jaguar very much. So I suppose you'll just have to stay here in its place."

Tory stepped back. Her lips were stiff. "You— what do you mean?"

"That you're going in the river with weights on your feet. It's not a hard death."

Unable to believe him, Tory felt numb, yet instinct sent her dodging back, looking for a weapon. "Brandy, theft is one thing. Murder's another."

"But I've killed before, my innocent." He laughed at her, stalking her like some sinuous great cat. "Remember at Uxmal? When you met me at that old ruin, I'd just cached a rare codex that a Mexican archaeologist and I happened to find at the same time a few miles from there. I doubt they've found his body yet—never may—but that was why I was eager to get back to Mérida."

"You—you're incredible!" Tory breathed.

Her groping hand found a shattered piece of stalactite. She crouched farther back into the weird configurations, meaning to fight to the last minute, hurt him all she could, scar his face and hands so he'd have explaining to do even though it'd be too late to help her.

Brandy sighed. "I'd rather not do this."

"You certainly don't have to! You can put the jaguar back and—"

"But there's the man I killed beyond Uxmal," Brandy finished. "And this jaguar I intend to carry out. Why fight, Victoria? You haven't a chance."

Tory gripped the crystalline sliver, prepared to shift sideways. Brandy started forward, his face a mask. Had she ever thought she knew him? Thought she loved him once?

"Hold it, Sherrod!"

Zan rose up from a pile of rock near the river. He had a gun, but Brandy reached for his, was squeezing the trigger when something *zanged*. An arrow quivered in his back and a second lodged beside it. Florentino and Don Luis rose from behind a farther pile of rock as Zan ran from his cover. Brandy crawled a few feet, bloody froth edging his lips, made choking incoherent sounds, convulsed, the arrows jerking spasmodically, straightened, shuddered violently, and was still.

Florentino stepped across the body, unwrapped the jaguar, waded out, and placed it on its niche.

Zan took Tory out while Florentino and Don Luis followed with the corpse. "I'm sorry," Zan said when they were outside the cavern. "We meant to take him alive, but Florentino had other plans."

"This was a trap?"

"Yes. That dead archaeologist's body was found, and it seemed likely to have been done by someone on the tour, someone who might be smuggling artifacts. I was asked to watch out, and of course I got Don Luis' help. What I was really scared of was that you were involved."

"And I was afraid you were."

Zan gave her a little shake. "When I saw you come out of that tunnel tonight, I could have howled! I thought you'd come to help Brandy. Then when I heard—he really would have killed you! What possessed you to follow him?"

"I thought I could get him to leave the jaguar."

Numbness began to wear off and Tory was shaking. She couldn't mourn Brandy. The man who'd died in the cave wasn't the man she'd thought she was in love with; he was an icy stranger, a man who'd already murdered for the sake of a thing he could sell. All the same, she couldn't keep from crying, soundlessly at first, then in wrenching sobs.

Zan put an arm around her, made her sit down outside the cavern, held her close till the others had gone down the trail to the village.

"Tory, this was an awful thing. I wish you hadn't seen it." His arms were strong and comforting. Tory buried her head on his shoulder and sobbed till dread and shock and pain lessened, till she could believe the wonder of being in Zan's arms.

He tilted up her face. "Dammit, I shouldn't! But—"

His mouth claimed hers for a long blissful moment. "I love you," he said. "Maybe it's too soon, maybe I should wait, but I can't! You have to know I love you. I've been wanting to say so ever since that first day."

"I love you," she said. "I knew it while I was following Brandy to the cavern."

Zan said softly, "Well, sweetheart, we can certainly do something about that." His lips took hers again, and the next thing he asked was whether they should get married in Mexico or go back to the States.

"Just so you're there," she said.

Big Bestsellers from SIGNET

☐ **LYNDON JOHNSON AND THE AMERICAN DREAM** by Doris Kearns. (#E7609—$2.50)

☐ **THIS IS THE HOUSE** by Deborah Hill. (#J7610—$1.95)

☐ **LORD RIVINGTON'S LADY** by Eileen Jackson. (#W7612—$1.50)

☐ **ROGUE'S MISTRESS** by Constance Gluyas. (#J7533—$1.95)

☐ **SAVAGE EDEN** by Constance Gluyas. (#J7171—$1.95)

☐ **LOVE SONG** by Adam Kennedy. (#E7535—$1.75)

☐ **THE DREAM'S ON ME** by Dotson Rader. (#E7536—$1.75)

☐ **SINATRA** by Earl Wilson. (#E7487—$2.25)

☐ **SUMMER STATION** by Maud Lang. (#E7489—$1.75)

☐ **THE WATSONS** by Jane Austen and John Coates. (#J7522—$1.95)

☐ **SANDITON** by Jane Austen and Another Lady. (#J6945—$1.95)

☐ **THE FIRES OF GLENLOCHY** by Constance Heaven. (#E7452—$1.75)

☐ **A PLACE OF STONES** by Constance Heaven. (#W7046—$1.50)

☐ **THE ROCKEFELLERS** by Peter Collier and David Horowitz. (#E7451—$2.75)

☐ **THE HAZARDS OF BEING MALE** by Herb Goldberg. (#E7359—$1.75)

More Big Bestsellers from SIGNET

☐ **COME LIVE MY LIFE** by Robert H. Rimmer.
(#J7421—$1.95)

☐ **THE FRENCHMAN** by Velda Johnston.
(#W7519—$1.50)

☐ **THE HOUSE ON THE LEFT BANK** by Velda Johnston.
(#W7279—$1.50)

☐ **A ROOM WITH DARK MIRRORS** by Velda Johnston.
(#W7143—$1.50)

☐ **KINFLICKS** by Lisa Alther.   (#E7390—$2.25)

☐ **RIVER RISING** by Jessica North.   (#E7391—$1.75)

☐ **THE HIGH VALLEY** by Jessica North. (#W5929—$1.50)

☐ **LOVER: CONFESSIONS OF A ONE NIGHT STAND** by Lawrence Edwards.   (#J7392—$1.95)

☐ **THE SURVIVOR** by James Herbert.   (#E7393—$1.75)

☐ **THE KILLING GIFT** by Bari Wood.   (#J7350—$1.95)

☐ **WHITE FIRES BURNING** by Catherine Dillon.
(#E7351—$1.75)

☐ **CONSTANTINE CAY** by Catherine Dillon.
(#W6892—$1.50)

☐ **FOREVER AMBER** by Kathleen Winsor.
(#J73( )—$1.95)

☐ **SMOULDERING FIRES** by Anya Seton.
(#J 76—$1.95)

☐ **HARVEST OF DESIRE** by Rochelle Larkin.
(#J7277—$1.95)

THE NEW AMERICAN LIBRARY, INC.,
P.O. Box 999, Bergenfield, New Jersey 07621

Please send me the SIGNET BOOKS I have checked above. I am enclosing $_____(check or money order—no currency or C.O.D.'s). Please include the list price plus 35¢ a copy to cover handling and mailing costs. (Prices and numbers are subject to change without notice.)

Name_____

Address_____

City_____State_____Zip Code_____
Allow at least 4 weeks for delivery